SECOND TO NONE

SECOND TO NONE

K.A. LINDE

ISBN-13: 978-1948427579

PART I

1

SAVANNAH
PRESENT

Coming here was a mistake.

I reflexively brought the end of my long black hair to my mouth. It was a habit I'd had since childhood. One I'd thought I'd cracked. Leave it to my mother to bring back all my bad habits.

"Anything else, Ms. Reynolds?" my driver asked as he lugged my Louis Vuitton luggage onto the sidewalk.

"No. Thank you. That will be all."

I passed him some cash and waited for him to drive away before returning my gaze to the mansion of my nightmares. I'd done everything in my power to get out from under the press of my mother's bad reputation. And somehow, I was right back where I'd started.

"Why did I agree to this again?" I grumbled under my breath as I hauled my luggage up the front walk.

My chest was heaving as I dropped the bags on the front porch. It didn't seem to matter how much I tried; cardio and I just did not get along. It sure didn't help that Savannah summers were oppressive on a good day. After living in LA for the last decade, my body wasn't used to the humidity. It felt more like I was drinking the air than breathing it. So, I waited until my heart rate dropped, swiping the bead of sweat off my brow, before knocking on the front door to Montgomery House.

The door swung inward, and my gorgeous, indominable mother stood in the entrance. Rebecca Charlotte Montgomery was a force. I was an actress, made my living pretending to be someone else, and was frequently called larger than life. But I had nothing on my mother.

"Josephine!" she said, her hand going to her chest. "You made it."

"I made it."

I could hardly keep from shaking my head at her. She wore a sheer floor-length pink robe with black edging over a corseted bathing suit. Her black hair was piled high on her head in a distinctly overly large Southern coif. And she had on fuzzy heeled slippers. She had a golden tan, indicative of our Mediterranean roots. I tanned that easily too. A dry martini with extra olives was in one hand.

"Come in, darling."

"Where am I staying?" I asked as I dragged the bags over the threshold and into the house where I'd spent every summer since childhood up to my senior year.

The air-conditioning hit me like a wave of relief. How did people live here before air-conditioning?

"Your old room, of course. Don't worry. I've had it renovated. You'll feel right at home."

Sure. Right at home. That was exactly how I'd describe the feeling of being back in my mother's house.

I swallowed back the words and took the stairs up to the second-floor landing. The bedroom I'd occupied over the summers growing up was unrecognizable. Gone was the ruffled bedspread and white four-poster bed and delicate, feminine touches. Now, the room could have belonged to a stranger. It could have been a bed-and-breakfast for all I knew. The comforter was stark white with a mountain of pale blue and gold throw pillows. Everything was new and modern, in contrast to how old the house was.

It felt like something I'd have back in LA. Not anything I'd expect in Savannah.

This house fucked me up.

My phone dinged, and I pulled it out to see a text from my dad.

Did you make it? See your mom yet? You know you don't have to stay there.

I forced a smile at my dad's concern. He and my mom hadn't been together since I had been in the womb. They'd never been much more than civil. When I'd told him I was staying here, he'd balked. I didn't blame him since my mother and I had never gotten along. But that was a long time ago.

I made it. I'm upstairs in my old room. Mom is mom. I'll be fine.

Get a hotel if she becomes too much. Love you.

Love you too.

I set one suitcase on a luggage rack and changed out of my traveling suit and into a purple dress and heels. After running a cool towel on my neck and wrists, I took a deep breath and headed back downstairs.

The mansion had six bedrooms and six and a half bathrooms. It had belonged to her husband's family for generations. She and Edward had never had children, and so, to everyone's chagrin, it had been bequeathed to her upon his death. Meanwhile, my dad and I had lived in the north Atlanta suburbs. He was an artist, and without the child support checks my mother had diligently given him for taking me off her hands nine months out of the year, we wouldn't have had a roof over our head. I'd hated always asking for money from my mother, but if I needed anything, it wasn't my dad who provided. On the flip side, it certainly wasn't my mother who had ever been there for me when it was important. Money didn't solve all problems.

"What do you think?" my mother asked when I entered the kitchen and found her shaking out another martini.

"It's ... modern."

"I thought it'd remind you of LA." She offered the drink to me. "Martini?"

"No thanks."

"Well, Josephine, do you want to use the pool or ..."

"Josie," I reminded her. While I went by Josephine professionally, I still wasn't used to anyone who really knew me calling me that. Even my mother.

She waved her hand at me. "I birthed you. I can call you what I want."

"Fine." I ground my teeth together. "And no, I'm going to head to the set."

"All right. Let me get you a key." She dropped her martini and reached in one of the kitchen drawers to retrieve a set of keys. "Gold one is to the front door. You can drive the Benz while you're here."

"I can Uber," I told her.

"Don't be silly. I have a garage of cars. Pick which one you want."

"Sure."

"And Josie," my mother said softly. Her eyes were earnest when I faced her again. "I'm glad you're staying here."

I shot her a half-smile. "I'll see you later."

She nodded, and I disappeared through the living room to the garage. I still had no idea why I'd agreed to this. The relationship was complicated. I had been in middle school when my mother's husband overdosed. She was the talk of the town for marrying one of the wealthiest men in Savannah, and her reputation turned to infamy after he died and she got every cent of his considerable fortune. Half of the town called her a gold digger and man-eater, and the other half said she killed him. I never knew what to believe, and my mother refused to speak on the subject. Couple that with her abandoning me with my dad—except for the summers, which I'd been coerced into spending with her—and we'd never gotten along.

I probably would have given up coming to Savannah

at all if my two best friends, Lila and Marley, weren't here. They were the closest thing I'd ever had to sisters.

And then there was Maddox.

I shook my head and popped the door on the Mercedes. I didn't want to think about Maddox. He was Marley's twin brother and still lived in Savannah. I was sure that I was going to see him while I was filming here for six weeks. But *complicated* didn't even begin to describe my relationship with him.

Putting Maddox out of my thoughts, I took the car down the narrow Savannah streets and out of town toward the filming studio. After starring in the hit teen supernatural-school show *Academy* for eight seasons, we'd been off the air for two years. Now, the studio had green-lit a follow-up full-length movie to close out the last chapter of the show. Fans had been clamoring for it since it'd ended. I hadn't been sure it was ever going to happen until I got the call a month ago.

I parked out front of the mostly empty studio. We didn't have to be here for another couple days, but I'd wanted to come home early. Lila and Marley were in Atlanta now but had promised to come visit. That had been enough to get me to agree. Any excuse to see my besties.

My favorite director, Jimmy, from the first eight seasons of *Academy* had gotten the job for the film. He'd called me personally and offered me my spot as Cassie Herrington again. As if they could make it without me.

I pulled the door open to the studio and entered a new world. Jimmy had mentioned some technological innovations, but truthfully, I hadn't listened too hard. I was busy memorizing my lines and digging deep back into my character. Jimmy had said he'd meet me at the studio to discuss it all before we got started.

But so far, I hadn't seen him.

"Josephine Reynolds," a voice said behind me.

I knew that voice. Oh God, I *knew* that voice.

I whipped around and found Maddox Nelson standing in the middle of the studio, wearing a gray T-shirt, molded to his ripped figure, and dark jeans. His usual messy, wild curls were cut short and slicked into order. His jaw was square and chiseled and those dark eyes ... they still went straight through me.

I hadn't seen him in a year and a half, and it hadn't exactly ended amicably.

Who was I kidding? It had gone up in flames and burned like a wildfire.

"Maddox," I whispered.

"Hey, Josie," he said with a smirk on his lips. "Surprise."

2

SAVANNAH
PRESENT

"What are you doing here?" I asked, frozen in place.

"Didn't you hear? I'm doing the visual effects."

The words were out of his mouth, and still, I didn't quite process them. Maddox was an incredibly talented animator. He'd started his career working with Pixar before creating his own company, MadSon Productions, and moving over to CGI for popular superhero movies. I'd never thought that he'd agree to work on something as small as an *Academy* movie.

"I ... I didn't hear." My voice quavered slightly, and I reached for the bravado that was my signature. But somehow, with Maddox, I just couldn't manage it anymore. "So, we'll be working together? Why didn't you tell me?"

"And miss the look on your face?" he said with a laugh. "Never."

He didn't say that we hadn't spoken in eighteen months. That neither of us had crossed that divide. That didn't need to be said. We both let it hang between us.

It didn't explain what he was doing here. Why he'd be here when I'd thought he never wanted to see me again. Which was hard enough, considering he was my best friend's twin brother.

"Well, this should be ... fun," I said, glancing around the room. "How can they afford you?"

He shrugged. "I had a break in my schedule. After a year off, we all wanted to get back to work. No matter what it was."

That I understood completely—2020 had felt like a decade. It was nice that my career was back up and running after the break. When Jimmy had called, I'd nearly jumped out of my seat. I was ready to be anywhere but stuck in my house in LA.

"True. I wasn't sure the *Academy* reboot was ever going to happen. Even though the fans begged for it."

He shrugged. "You have a huge fan base."

It was hard not to smile when I thought about everything that *Academy* had given me. Eight full seasons, an Emmy for best actress, and a rabid fan base that adored me. I could never thank them enough for how I'd gotten here.

"There's my favorite person!" a man crowed behind me.

A smile split my face, and I found Jimmy Torsney striding toward me. "Jimmy," I cried, throwing my arms around him.

He picked me up and swung me around in place. When he set me back down on my feet, his smile was wide and welcoming. "Girl, look at your skinny ass. Having a gym in your house sure paid off."

I laughed. "Wasn't much else to do."

"The boys are going to be salivating over you," he said. He winked at Maddox. "The straight ones at least."

Maddox kept a straight face through Jimmy's antics. He was always like this. The one non-creepy director we'd had, who always had our back when a producer got too handsy.

"Don't sell me short, Jimmy," I teased. "The girls will be into me too." I twirled in place for him. My purple skirt flying in a circle around my thighs. This was the Josephine Reynolds that had gotten a lead actress position at twenty-two after never acting before in her life. It was so much easier being her when Maddox wasn't looking on.

"She's right, you know," Jimmy agreed. "Well, to business then. I see you've met our visual effects guy. Maddox Nelson is the best in the business. We are beyond lucky to have him."

"Thanks, Jimmy," Maddox said. His eyes shot back to mine. My insides turned to jelly in that one quick glance.

"I won't let you be modest," Jimmy said, slinging arms around both of our shoulders and directing us toward the massive structure at the center of the studio. "From eight seasons of *Academy* to this film, it's going to be night and day. Night and day!" He grinned broadly at me. "We're elevating everything to the next level, and it's all because of this guy."

Maddox eased out of his embrace. "Should be fun."

"Fun." Jimmy laughed. "He's talking state-of-the-art graphics technology that he *invented*, and it's fun. Love this guy."

Maddox just shrugged. Unlike me, he had no bravado. He was a genius. As much as his sister, who was currently faculty at Emory University in neuroscience and genetics, doing research on dementia. But Maddox used his genius as an artist. He'd revolutionized visual effects.

"Do you know he has an Oscar?" Jimmy said, slapping Maddox's chest. "Two actually!"

Maddox arched an eyebrow at me.

I plastered on a smile. "I'd heard."

"Josie and I actually know each other already," Maddox admitted.

"You've worked on something together?" Jimmy asked. His smile was bright. "I didn't know that."

"We grew up together actually," I said before he could think too closely on the fact that I hadn't gotten any real work other than *Academy*. I didn't count the handful of commercials and one horrid failure of an indie film.

"Well, look at that. Old friends reunited. I forgot that you're from Savannah." Jimmy nodded his head. "This feels right. Going to be a great movie. Martin gets in on Friday. You should take everyone out to see the town before we get started."

I didn't miss the slight flinch Maddox made at the mention of Martin Harper—my costar ... and ex-husband. Just the person he wanted to spend time with after work.

"Sure," I agreed.

Maddox said nothing.

"Good. Good. I'll leave you to it. Maddox, if you need anything, let me know. Josie," he said, pointing at me, "your trailer is all set up. Josephine Reynolds in big bold letters. Just like you like it. See you bright and early Monday morning."

Jimmy waved us off and headed to his next mission, leaving Maddox and me all alone once more.

"Well, I should probably get back to work too," Maddox said. "Lots to do before we get you in there."

But I wasn't ready for him to go. It didn't matter what had happened between us or how we'd fallen apart the last decade. I still didn't want him to go.

"Did you finish the renovations on Gran's house?"

He startled. "How'd you know I was renovating?"

"Marley," I said softly.

"Right. Of course." He nodded. "Yeah. I just finished. Took a full year, but it's done. Still feels like Gran and Gramps's house, but it needed the upgrade."

"I bet it's so satisfying."

"You have no idea," he said, animation coming back to his face.

"I'd love to see it."

His face shuttered at that. "Yeah. Where are you staying? You get a hotel or something?"

I breathed out heavily. "I'm staying at my mom's."

His eyes widened. He blurted out the question seemingly before he could stop himself, "Why?"

"I keep asking myself that question. I called to tell her about the show, and she asked me to stay with her."

"And you agreed?"

"She seemed sincere. I'm kind of kicking myself right now. She greeted me with a martini."

"Of course she did," he said with a soft laugh.

My chest ached at that sound. I'd missed it.

"Maddox," I said, biting on my hair nervously.

"Old habits, Jos." He caught the piece of hair and pulled it out of my mouth.

My body went still at his nearness. Our eyes met. He looked away first.

I swallowed. "Are we going to be okay for the next six weeks here?"

"At work?" He shrugged. "Sure."

"And outside of work?"

He sighed. "Josie ..."

"We've been friends our entire lives."

"Friends," he said darkly.

"You know what I mean," I rushed on.

"Unfortunately, I do." His gaze shifted away from me.

I ground my teeth together. "Why did you even take this job then?" I couldn't keep the heat out of my voice. The old Josie shooting to the surface. "You knew it was my movie. You knew I'd be the lead. You knew I'd be here, in your city, for six weeks. All of that, and you didn't tell me. Why would you do all of this, Maddox, if you were just going to avoid me the whole time?"

"What do you want me to say?" he demanded, fury creeping into his voice.

"I'm trying to understand what you're doing here if you clearly don't want anything to do with me."

"Not everything is about you, Josie."

I huffed. "I wish things could go back to the way they were. We don't have to be enemies when we were always more."

"Well, that's wishful thinking."

I closed my eyes and sighed heavily. "You didn't miss me?"

Maddox stepped forward, brushing my dark hair off my face. I met his dark eyes. "I missed you." I listed toward him at those words. His eyes dipped to my mouth, as if at any moment, he might claim what rightfully belonged to him. "But that doesn't change anything. And we both know it."

When he stepped back, putting even more distance between us than before, I felt as cold as ice. The second of emotion in his eyes when we'd been within kissing distance had disappeared. Somehow, he could hide his emotions even better than the actress in that moment. And we'd done this to each other. I'd taught him how to harden himself as much as he'd taught me to open up. We were both reaping what we'd sowed.

"I'm going to get back to work," Maddox said. He took one last look, almost drinking me in, before walking away.

And I let him go.

Something was broken between us. One conversation wasn't going to fix years of damage. But I hadn't realized how much I wanted it to until I saw him.

If only we could go back to when we'd both been young and innocent and redo it all. If only ...

3

SAVANNAH

MARCH 29, 2005

"You made it!" Lila cried. My best friend dashed out of the front door of Marley's house, throwing her arms around me.

I laughed and caught her head-on. "I made it!"

The person who completed our trio, Marley, hopped down the front sidewalk. "It's about time."

"It's a four-hour drive!" I shoved at her shoulder and then pulled her into a hug.

"You should have come last night."

"I wanted to, but you bitches were busy." I shrugged.

It hadn't been my fault that I couldn't drive down to Savannah from my home in Atlanta the day before. My spring break had started Friday afternoon, and Dad had said I could leave whenever I wanted. But Marley had been working at the dance studio all weekend, and Lila's mom, Deb, had made her be involved in all the Catholic church activities for Easter. Deb had started working for the church, and she'd forced Lila into the all-girls Catholic school, St. Catherine's, when tuition was waived.

Lila wasn't even Catholic, but it was the best school in town.

"Yeah, yeah," Marley said. "At least you're here now."

"And I am ready to get down to Tybee."

Marley shivered. "It's not even going to be warm enough to tan."

"Does it look like I care?"

"Maddox is already there with his friends," Lila said as she tugged her long blonde hair up into a ponytail. "Get changed, and we'll go."

"Are we taking the minivan?" I asked. We joked about the car, but as much as Marley hated that Gran and Gramps had given her a minivan for her sixteenth birthday, she loved having her own wheels.

Marley rolled her eyes as she stomped back toward her house. "Can't we take your BMW?"

"And get sand everywhere?" I scoffed. "No thanks."

Marley was muttering under her breath about where I could stick sand. Lila caught my eye, and we both burst into laughter. I lugged out the duffel bag I'd filled mostly with bathing suits and cosmetics and then followed, shooting out a text to Dad.

Just got to Marley's house. Love you.

Are you going to see your mom?

Not if I can help it.

Your choice, Jos. Check in now and then.

Sure Dad.

I pocketed my phone with a grin. My dad never cared that much where I was or what I was doing. Not when it meant he got to spend the entire week of spring break in his studio, creating his precious artwork.

"Where's Gran?" I asked once I dropped my bag in Marley's room.

Marley shrugged. "She went somewhere to volunteer. Gave me a twenty and told me to have my phone nearby at all times or I was grounded and you couldn't stay here."

"Sounds right."

I was used to Gran's overprotective behavior. Marley and Maddox had been raised by their grandma and grandpa, and they were *strict*. I still thought it was better than my situation, which included zero adult supervision. Or more accurately ... zero adults who gave a single fuck what I was doing at any given point in time.

But I certainly wasn't going to break any rules. Deb would probably let me stay with Lila, but it might be just as likely that she'd send me to stay with my mother. Deb was eternally charitable and never believed any of the baser rumors about my mother. I wasn't sure which ones I thought were true, but I knew that I didn't want to see her if I didn't have to.

So, I changed out of my travel clothes and into a bikini and a teeny-tiny cover-up. Then, the three of us piled into Marley's minivan and careened toward Tybee Island.

"I still wish we could have made the Florida beach trip work," Lila said.

Marley pursed her lips and gripped the steering wheel tighter. "Tell me about it."

"One day, we'll all make the trip."

"I doubt Gran will ever let me go on an unsupervised trip to Florida. I'll be thirty, and she'll still be dictating my life."

I snorted. "And I thought I was the drama queen. We'll do it in college or something. We'll have just as much fun hanging out this week. We can go to Tybee every day. It might not be as warm as Florida, but we will make it work."

Marley shot me an appreciative look. I was just glad to spend the time with my two best friends. The girls back in Atlanta were all at Florida beaches unsupervised. I could have gone with any of them on the trip, but I hadn't wanted to go without Mars and Lila.

A half hour later, through the marshy islands that surrounded Savannah, we made it to Tybee Island. It wasn't quite Florida, but it had miles of sandy, pebbled beaches and a boardwalk. We used to beg Gran to drive us out here every summer to build sandcastles and devour low-country boil at a local beachside shack. Just thinking about it made my mouth water.

Marley tossed me her phone. "Check where Maddox parked."

I scrolled to the text chat with Maddox. "13th Street."

Marley pulled down 13th a few minutes later. She parked behind her brother's pickup truck. I hopped out of the minivan and went to the machine to feed it cash for our stay.

The three of us headed toward the bridge that passed over the dunes leading to the beach. I grabbed for my Ray-Bans as the sun beat down on our shoulders. We were lucky that it was unseasonably warm. It had been in the sixties all weekend, but it was high seventies today and even supposed to hit the eighties tomorrow.

We trekked down the beach until we found Maddox throwing a Frisbee with a few guys I'd never met before. But I barely paid them any mind. My eyes were locked on Maddox.

I'd known him since we had been kids. I'd always known he was into me, and I flirted with him relentlessly because of that fact, but I wasn't supposed to have any feelings toward Maddox. He was Marley's twin, and we'd practically grown up together. But something had happened between coming into town for his sixteenth birthday over Halloween and today. He was ... hot.

He was shirtless and in a pair of cerulean-blue board shorts that stopped just above his knee. My eyes traveled down the washboard abs that I'd never seen look this good before. His mess of brown curls bounced as he ran forward and tossed a Frisbee to one of his friends. He ran a hand back through his hair, and I saw a defined bicep before he caught sight of me.

Maddox stopped dead in his tracks. His eyes lit up as they traveled over my bare shoulders, down my skimpy, strapless cover-up, to my long, tan legs. He opened and closed his mouth a few times, dumbstruck.

Then, the Frisbee hit him squarely in his chest.

He guffawed as he faltered backward a step, and the Frisbee landed in the sand. My hand flew to my mouth. His friends, Marley, and Lila all laughed.

"Pay attention, dipshit," one of his friends called, jogging over to him.

Maddox rubbed his chest reflexively. "Maybe call my name next time."

"I did," the guy said. He slapped him on the back and picked up the Frisbee, shooting it back out.

Maddox headed over to us as we laid our towels out. I stripped out of my dress, leaving me in nothing but my hot-pink string bikini. Maddox was staring again, his mouth slightly agape.

"You're going to let in flies," Marley snapped at him, brushing her own dark curls out of her face.

He quickly shut his mouth, a hint of pink at his cheeks. "You made it to town."

"Yep. It was an easy drive."

"I'm glad."

His friend followed him, wrapping an arm across Maddox's shoulders and leaning forward. "You going to introduce me to your girl?"

"She's not ..." Maddox started, eyes wide. "She's, uh, just ..."

"Philip Kearney," Marley chided.

Lila knocked her hip into him. "Surely, you've met our friend Josie? She's here every summer."

"Oh, *this* is Josie," he said with a smirk in Maddox's direction.

Maddox's jaw worked. "Hey, Josie."

"Maddox." I smiled at him.

I wasn't embarrassed by everything going on. As much as Marley hated people noticing her for anything but her big brain, I was perfectly okay with these guys stumbling all over themselves over me.

Even Maddox.

"Let's get back to the game!" one of the other guys called.

Philip yanked on Maddox's arm. "Come on, dude."

Maddox met my gaze for a split second longer before following his friend back into the sand.

I flopped down onto my towel and spread suntan oil with minimal SPF all over my body. Marley still looked irritated, but she was busy putting up an umbrella, so that she could promptly hide her soon-to-be lobster skin.

Lila snagged the tanning oil from me and slathered up her legs. "I know what that look means."

"What look?" I asked conspiratorially.

But I was still watching Maddox run up and down the beach.

Lila flipped the bottle at me. "You know how Maddox feels about you."

"Do I?"

"Don't even think about it, Josie," Marley said, sitting down underneath the umbrella and dropping her giant beach hat over her curls.

"Think about what?"

"That's my brother. My twin brother. And I know how you are with boys."

I put my hand to my chest. "*Moi*?"

Lila snorted. "*Love 'em and leave 'em* is practically your motto."

"Do not break my poor little brother's heart. He has all that artist angst. I could not deal with it." Marley's eye roll was definitely exaggerated, but her words were for real. "He'd probably write a song about you."

I sighed. "Okay. I will stay away from him," I promised. And flirt my ass off. "But I can still appreciate that he's gotten hot this year."

Marley groaned, and Lila just cackled.

I tied my black hair into a messy bun on the top of my head and lay back against the towel. The sand was warm. The sky was blue. The sound of the waves lulled me. This wasn't the spring break I'd planned, but I was at the beach with my friends and had cute boys to look at. I couldn't ask for more.

Except for maybe a cute boy to kiss ...

4

SAVANNAH

APRIL 1, 2005

"And who is going to be at this party?" Gran asked.

Maddox sighed. "It's not a party, Gran. It's me and Philip watching a movie."

"Are Philip's parents going to be there?"

"I don't know. I think so."

"Any girls?"

"Gran," he groaned.

"Don't *Gran* me," she warned. "Your grades slipped this semester, Maddox. If you used your brain half as much as your sister, we wouldn't need to have this conversation."

"My grades are fine. The teachers just want me to show my work, and that's stupid."

"Yet you manage to get perfect scores in your art classes."

Maddox huffed. "Because that's actually interesting."

Gran sighed heavily, as if this was a conversation she'd had on more than one occasion. Marley and Maddox were both off the charts in intellect. Marley focused on academics, but Maddox only put his focus on his passions. Mars had complained about it enough for me to know where this was leading.

"If you start showing your work, I'll start letting you go to these things," Gran said.

"Okay. If I agree to show my work, can I go?"

"You'd better hold up your end of the deal," Gran said.

"I will," he said swiftly. Anything to get to go.

"I want to speak with Philip's parents before I agree to this," she said.

I stood at the top of the stairs, waiting to see if Maddox got approval for us to go to his friend's to watch a movie. He stomped up the stairs a few minutes later in a huff.

"Well?" I asked.

He shrugged with a twitch in his jaw. "She's calling his parents."

"Wow. She cares so much."

Dad wouldn't have even asked who was going to be there or what time I'd be back or if there were parents. The weekend before coming here, I'd gone to a house party. I'd gotten high with some random dudes I'd met at the basketball game and people were giving blow jobs in the bathroom.

He snorted. "Too much. It's just a movie."

"Must be nice," I muttered.

"I promise, it just sucks."

"If you say so."

We'd gotten home from the beach a few hours ago as the temperatures dropped. Marley and Lila had to be at the dance studio for competition prep all night. They'd be there late, and I wanted nothing less than to go to my mother's house. When Philip had invited us to come to his house and watch the latest movie release he'd rented, I'd jumped at the opportunity before thinking about whether or not Gran would even let us out of the house.

A few minutes later, Gran called Maddox down the stairs.

Then, Maddox stuck his head in the stairway. He gave me a thumbs-up. I jumped to my feet and trotted down the stairs after him. We waved good-bye to Gran, hurried into his truck, and pulled away.

"I can't believe she let us go," Maddox said. "I thought she'd stop us."

"Me too. It's kind of exciting. Back home, no one gives a shit where I am or what I'm doing."

Maddox frowned. "Your dad probably cares."

I shook my head. "He's too busy at the art studio. Sometimes he forgets he has a daughter."

"That's sad."

"It's whatever," I said dismissively. "So, what are we actually doing at Philip's house? Did someone pick up some weed, or should we use my fake to get some beer?"

Maddox did a double take. "Uh ... we're going to watch a movie."

I blinked at him. "Seriously? Like ... actually watch a movie?"

He laughed. "Uh, yeah. What kind of parties are you going to in Atlanta?"

My cheeks heated. "The wrong kind."

Maddox parked in Philip's driveway, where a handful

of other cars were already parked on the street. I slid out of the truck and followed him around back to the basement door. Maddox pushed his way inside, and we took the stairs down to a dark game room, filled with old couches, a projection TV, and tons of board games.

"You made it," Philip said, shaking hands with Maddox. "And you brought Josie."

I winked at him. "He couldn't have left without me."

"Of that I'm sure. Let me introduce you around."

There were about a dozen people already crowded around the couches or digging through a mini fridge. I recognized some of the guys from the beach and was glad to see a few girls were also there. I accepted a Coke from Philip and took a seat on the last open couch. Maddox dropped down next to me with a Dr. Pepper in hand.

"All the movies out this month were shit," Philip said as he slid a DVD into the player. "But the new Natalie Portman stripper movie just came out."

I rolled my eyes. "Typical. It's called *Closer*, and it's a goddamn masterpiece."

"It was nominated for two Oscars," Maddox said.

"Right. Natalie Portman and Clive Owen put on the most incredible performance."

"And the way it's shot," Maddox added. "I saw some of the clips, and it's visually perfect."

"They were robbed."

"Can we not with the film bullshit, Mad Son?" Philip said.

I glanced at him in confusion. "*Mad* Son?"

Maddox sighed. "Maddox Nelson. Mad from my first

name and Son from my last name. It's just what he calls me."

"Ridiculous."

"It's the best!" Philip said. "Now shut up."

Then he pressed play on the movie.

I'd seen *Closer* opening weekend. I'd bought a ticket to see *National Treasure* and then slipped into *Closer* to experience the rated-R film. It had enraptured me. The four people who moved in and out of each other's lives, wrecking everything in their path in the need for love. Somehow, I felt connected to that. Like I could understand the extremes they'd go to feel something.

The last light was flicked off, and Natalie Portman walked onto the screen. I leaned back in my seat, hypnotized all over again. But watching it with Maddox seated next to me was a whole new experience. His hip was pressed tight against mine. Our shoulders touched. Heat radiated off our bodies. I chanced a glance up at him and found he was already staring down at me.

He startled and hastily dragged his eyes back to the screen. I flushed and looked away too. It didn't matter that I dated a lot back home. It was different with him.

Halfway through the movie, the rest of the couples were all making out. Philip was making some rude comments about Natalie's infamous stripper performance. Maddox rolled his eyes and adjusted his seat, which somehow put us even closer together.

Then, I looked up at him again. He flushed but didn't look away.

"What?" I whispered.

"I like you like this."

I arched an eyebrow. "How?"

"Passionate. I know how much you love films."

And I did. My dad had gotten me a collection of black-and-white movies, and I watched them until I could quote them backward and forward. I might have been a drama queen, but it was because I'd been born in the wrong era. I should have been a black-and-white star. I still couldn't get over the desperate feeling I'd gotten the first time I saw *Casablanca* or the thrill of seeing myself in *A Letter to Three Wives.*

"I do," I finally said.

Then, Maddox's hand covered mine, where it lay against my thigh. My stomach flipped as sparks shot up my arm at that one touch. When I didn't immediately pull away, he turned my hand over in his and drew circles into my palm before threading our fingers together.

A shiver went through me at the contact. And I could see how much he wanted to kiss me. I could let him. But I'd promised Marley that I wouldn't break her brother's heart. I should show him that I wasn't interested, but I didn't want to stop either even though I knew it couldn't work when I was four hours away.

So when he slipped an arm around my shoulders, I fit my body against him, laying my head against his chest. His other hand went to my knee. I wasn't used to guys who went this slow either. Guys back home would have had that hand up my skirt and tried to drag me out of the party a minute later.

Maddox was slow. This meant something to him. And it made butterflies erupt in my stomach. I'd never felt this way when I was with anyone else. I'd always gone along with things because the guy was hot, and why not? It hadn't occurred to me to care whether or not I could fall in love with them.

I was realizing how stupid all of that had been.

Was this what it was supposed to feel like?

The thought scared me. Maddox was here. I was in Atlanta. I'd be back in the summer, but that wasn't how relationships worked, and there was Marley to contend with.

Suddenly, I couldn't concentrate on one of my favorite movies anymore. All I could hear was Maddox's rapid heart rate in my ear. And how good it felt to be in his arms. And how much I needed to stop this from going any further.

When the movie finished, I got to my feet and retreated to the bathroom to calm my own racing pulse. Maddox waited for me at the basement door, and after saying our good-byes and receiving a knowing look from Philip, we got back into his truck.

He didn't start the truck immediately. He just sat there, clearly trying to work up the right words to say.

"That was fun. Different than what I'm used to at home."

"I had fun too." His dark eyes were set on my face. "With you."

His hand found mine in the dark. He drew me closer against him. I swallowed. My heart was pounding. I shouldn't do this. I couldn't give him what he wanted.

"Josie," he whispered into the night.

And I knew exactly what he wanted with that look. I could see every single thing he was thinking. It would be so easy to give in to that. To lean forward and press my lips against his. But where exactly was this going? We were sixteen, and he was four hours away. And no matter what my body wanted, Maddox wasn't the kind of guy I could have a fling with.

"We should probably get home," I said, scooting back before he could go through with that kiss. "Marley will be home soon."

Hurt flashed across his features. "Right. Sure." He started his truck and pulled out of Philip's driveway.

He didn't say anything when we got back to Gran's. Just shot me one more look, filled with longing that I had to ignore. Pretending I want that kiss was one of the hardest things I'd ever done.

I half-expected him to drag me to him and steal the kiss he wanted. But Maddox wasn't that kind of guy. He didn't steal what didn't belong to him. He had no clue that I would be more than willing to go along with it. Years of friendship stayed his hand.

Marley looked between us distrustfully. It wasn't until we were up in her room with the lights off that she asked, "Did you and Maddox hook up?"

"No," I said quickly.

"Did he try?"

I hesitated. "No."

"I'm shocked. Be careful with him, okay? You know he's in love with you."

I hid my secret smile. "Yeah, I'll be careful."

She didn't say anything else, but I spent way too long awake, imagining what it would be like to kiss someone who was actually in love with me.

5

SAVANNAH

SEPTEMBER 1, 2007

"**M**an, it's too busy to be at the beach."

Two years after that hope-filled spring break, I flopped backward on the towel and brought my wide-brimmed hat over my face. It made it so I couldn't see the hundreds of people that had congregated on Tybee Island, but it did nothing to block the noise. The beach was my happy place, and they were ruining it.

"Words I never thought I'd hear out of your mouth," Maddox said.

"I don't like it when it's this busy."

We'd spent all summer with Lila and Marley at the beach. But they were safely away at their respective colleges. It was just me and Maddox left behind. We wouldn't start at Savannah College of Art and Design until next week. And Labor Day on Tybee was *packed*.

Maddox chuckled. "You love people, Jos."

"True. But tourists," I groused.

"Fuck tourists."

I smirked and pushed back my hat to catch a glimpse

of him in a beach chair with his sketchbook balanced on one knee. Charcoal darkened his fingertips, and his eyes were intent on the page. Sometimes glancing up at our surroundings before dropping back down.

"What are you working on today?"

He caught my look, and his cheeks flushed. "Nothing."

"Your fingers are dipped in black. That's not nothing."

He shrugged. "It sort of sucks."

But when he flipped the page, it was far from nothing, and it definitely did not suck. It was a perfect rendering of me lying on the towel. One leg propped up, the other flat, the line of my exposed stomach, the curve of my shoulder. Even the hat obscuring my face. The background empty of tourists. Waves crashing in deceptively close.

My breath hitched. "Wow, Maddox. That's incredible."

"Nah, it's nothing. Just brushing up on my skills before I get into drawing classes this semester."

When I'd gotten into SCAD, I'd sat on the floor of my kitchen and sobbed with relief. There were great film programs all over the country, but I'd wanted SCAD more than anything. I called Marley to let her know, and Maddox was in the room. He'd gotten his acceptance letter the same day. With a full scholarship, of course. Dad had gone apoplectic at the price of tuition to an art private school for me, but I was lucky that my mother had agreed to pay for my education. Not that it made Dad any happier. We'd been living off of my mother's child support checks long enough. I knew Dad wished that he could support us more fully. That we didn't have to rely on Mom. But my shitty grades hadn't gotten me a full ride anywhere.

"You're probably already way ahead of everyone anyway."

Maddox shrugged. Eternally modest. "Maybe."

"You took visual effects classes at SCAD the last two semesters," I said with a shake of my head.

"Not for credit," he mumbled. I flung my hat at him. He caught it with a laugh. "What?"

"You need some of your sister's confidence."

"Ah, you think I should walk around and tell everyone that I'm smarter than them?"

"Sometimes!"

Maddox shut the sketchbook and tossed it back into his bag, dropping the charcoal at the bottom. "It doesn't make me any better than anyone else. And I'm not trying to cure an incurable disease, like Mars."

"No, but I bet you're going to do just as much in whatever pursuit you put your mind to," I argued. "You got a perfect SAT *and* ACT score. You could have gone wherever you wanted and cured diseases too." He wrinkled his nose. "Exactly. That's not what you want. It's not what I want either."

"You need to pass your science classes to do that, Jos."

I smacked his leg. "Hey! I passed."

With a C, but it was a pass. Math and science were not my forte. Debate? I'd been awesome at that. And drama? So much better than numbers.

He snorted. "Come on. Let's get out of here. If you're done, then I'm craving some Leopold's."

I grinned broadly. "Now you're speaking my language."

After throwing everything in my bag and tossing my towel over my shoulder, I followed Maddox to his truck. We put everything in the backseat, and then Maddox opened my door for me. I slid against the hot brown leather, hissing as the heated seat burned my bare skin.

"Sorry. Sorry." Maddox dropped a towel across the seat. I slid it under my butt and sank back down.

"Damn, that is on fire."

"Yeah. Summers and leather do not go together."

Maddox got into the driver's side, rolled the windows down, and headed back toward Savannah. I leaned my head out the window, letting the wind cool the sweat off my skin. Maddox's air-conditioning was intermittent at best. We could have taken my BMW, but there had been a crime spree the last couple weeks, and Maddox had said no one would break into his junker.

I cut a glance at him. He'd grown a handful of inches since the year before. Now, he was easily over six feet tall. His curls were wind-whipped, and those dark eyes were intent on the road ahead. He'd tugged a heather-gray T-shirt over his muscular torso, but I'd gotten my fill all afternoon.

Maddox and I had danced around this thing between us since that night over spring break. Marley had made her thoughts about it clear. So I'd always stayed away, but I knew that Maddox still had feelings for me. He was much worse at hiding it than I was.

"What are you looking at?" he asked, sliding his eyes to mine with an arched eyebrow.

I winked at him. "I like that shirt."

His throat bobbed. "It's just a T-shirt."

"Yeah, but it shows off your muscles."

He shot me a disbelieving look. "My muscles?"

I wrapped a hand around his bicep. "Have you been working out?"

Maddox huffed. "You're a relentless flirt."

"Obviously."

"You know you don't have to do that with me."

I jerked backward in my seat. Maddox knew as well as I did that the flirting was more a defense mechanism than anything. When I really liked someone, the bravado fell away, and I was just me. It was what had happened senior year with my first real boyfriend, Brandt. But he got to know the real Josie under the over-the-top behavior and promptly ditched me for someone else. Except he hadn't told me before getting high and sleeping with some strange girl at a party. Someone had recorded it or else I wouldn't have even known. I'd put up even more barriers after that.

"Just ... sort of happens," I muttered, looking out across the marsh as we crossed through Whitemarsh Island and back toward home.

Maddox didn't say anything else as we moved into downtown. I cursed when I saw the line to Leopold's.

"Holidays," Maddox grumbled. "Hop out, and I'll park."

I grabbed my wallet, stuffing it into the back pocket of my shorts, before jumping out of the truck and getting into line. It was going to be at least an hour wait. We could probably give up and find something else, but Leopold's was the best in town.

Twenty minutes later, I found Maddox scouring the line. I waved at him, and he took the spot next to me.

"Parking was a nightmare."

"When isn't it?"

When we finally got to the front of the line, Maddox pulled the door open for me. I sighed in relief at the air-conditioning.

Maddox rested his hand on the small of my back. "What'll you have?"

It was the small things with Maddox.

The look that said he knew exactly who I was. The smirk on his lips when I got him to loosen up. The Southern gentleman in him that opened my doors and walked on the outside of the sidewalk and offered me his coat when I was cold. Guys were just not raised like this in Atlanta.

"I'll have a Savannah Socialite."

Maddox shook his head. "Of course you will."

It was my mother who was the Savannah socialite, but the ice cream was to die for. Milk and dark chocolate ice cream with roasted pecans and bourbon caramel.

"I'll take a banana split," Maddox ordered.

I took my cone and stepped down to the end of the line to pay, but Maddox was already there, handing over some cash and dropping a tip into the jar.

"You didn't have to pay." Even if I was secretly happy.

"I've been working a lot."

He took his banana split, and we walked back into the heat. There weren't seats in front of the ice cream shop.

So, we turned north toward Reynolds Square. We dropped onto a bench under the Spanish moss. Despite the thousands of tourists in the city this weekend, the squares always felt like I'd been transported back in time to when Savannah was first constructed on a grid system.

"Your square is my favorite," Maddox said.

I laughed softly and licked the dripped ice cream from my cone. When we had been younger, I'd claimed Reynolds Square as my own. "Josephine Reynolds Square," I'd proclaimed for all to hear.

"Mine too."

"What's your plan after this?"

I shrugged. "Anything but going home."

"Don't want to see your mom?"

"Would you want to see yours?"

Maddox cringed and ditched the empty ice cream tray in a trash can. "Not particularly."

Marley and Maddox had been left at their Gran and Gramps's house at the age of two. Their mother only showed up when she needed money in between the guys she was seeing. She'd never been a mother to either of them. We had that in common.

"Are you going back to Atlanta to see your dad before school starts?"

I sighed and shrugged. "Yeah. I have to finish packing, and Dad is going to drive me down for move-in. He's so excited. But I'm worried about him."

"Why?"

"Only-child thing. Plus ..." I bit my lip and cut myself off.

"What?"

"It's nothing."

"Doesn't sound like nothing."

He was right. It was important, and I worried about my dad. I loved him, but he was relentless in the pursuit of his art and little else.

"I just worry about him. After I leave, he won't have child support checks anymore. It'll be hard on him."

Maddox squeezed my hand and then seemed to realize he'd done it and pulled back. "That's a lot to take on yourself. Your dad will make it work."

"I hope so," I said, clearing my throat. "Is Gran expecting you back?"

He shook his head. He looked no more ready to leave than I did. "We could head to the River Walk."

"I'll buy you a Wet Willie's."

He rolled his eyes. "We don't have to drink to have a good time."

"No, but it sure is fun. Plus, alcoholic *slushies*."

"I have to drive, and Gran would kill me."

"True," I said with a laugh. "But when we're at SCAD, I will convince you to get one."

"I heard SCAD is all house parties."

I shrugged. "Fine. I'll get you drunk at a house party."

He rolled his eyes again, but he was smiling as we headed out of the square. We took Abercorn to Bay Street and down the atrociously steep stone steps that led down to River Street. I was glad that I was in sandals on the walk down. Girls took the steps like fawns. Their ankles teetering and nearly collapsing the entire way down.

The sun was low on the horizon, painting the sky over the Savannah River a kaleidoscope of pink and orange. I leaned forward against the railing and watched the tourists pile onto the sunset paddleboat tour.

"I wish I had my sketchbook with me," Maddox said thickly.

I turned to face him. "Why?"

He stepped forward, bridging the distance between us. "Because you look beautiful."

I swallowed, chewing on my hair to keep from reaching for him. I couldn't do this with Maddox. I'd told Marley that I wouldn't do anything with him. I'd made that promise in good faith. No matter how hard it had been to keep my word when we spent all summer together.

"What are you nervous about?" he asked, tentatively reaching forward and drawing the hair out of my mouth.

"We can't do this."

He arched an eyebrow and moved closer still. "Why not?"

"I promised Marley."

Now, his eyebrows shot straight up. "Promised her what exactly?"

"That I'd stay away from you."

"Did you need to stay away from me?" A step closer. So close. Kissably close.

"Yes," I whispered. I tipped my head back to look up into his dark eyes. "Remember spring break sophomore year? When we went to Philip's party and almost kissed?"

"Yeah. I figured you didn't want to. I stayed away after that because I didn't want to make you uncomfortable."

"I wasn't. I just ... didn't want to hurt you or my friendship with Mars." I glanced away, crossing my arms over my chest. I'd never had a moment like this with a guy before. I'd never had anyone else in my life like Maddox before either.

Maddox tipped my chin up, so I was looking up into his face again. "Josie, did you *want* to kiss me?"

"Yes," I forced out.

"Do you want to kiss me now?"

He didn't wait for my answer. The word was already on my lips and clear on my face. I'd wanted nothing more than to kiss Maddox Nelson for two long years.

He tugged me tight against him and crushed our lips together. All the timidity fell off his shoulders as he took control of me. He'd been holding back more than I had, judging by the passion in his kiss. The slant of that mouth against mine that sent butterflies thwacking away in my stomach. The grip of his hands as he slid one hand around my waist and the other up into my hair.

A soft moan escaped my lips at the first brush of his tongue against mine. He tasted sweet from the ice cream. The feeling was like I was sinking into a down comforter. Like I'd always been meant to be in this moment.

I hadn't realized that I was clutching on to his shirt for dear life. I slung my arms around his neck, threading my fingers through the curly strands at the nape. I'd wondered what it would be like to run my fingers through the unruly mess. I'd mussed them before, but this was wholly different.

Every part of this kiss was wholly different.

Body, mind, and soul, I belonged right here on the River Walk with this man.

A whistle broke us apart with a soft laugh.

"Guess we were giving them a show," I said softly. My lips swollen and cheeks flushed.

"Let 'em see."

"Since when did you become a rebel?"

"Since the girl of my dreams was in my arms."

A rush of emotion hit my chest at those words. The girl of his dreams. No one had ever talked to me like that.

I rested my head against his chest as he drew me in closer. We swayed slightly as the sun fully sank below the skyline. I didn't know where this was going or what was coming next. Next week, we'd both be at SCAD with a whole new college experience before us. Anything could happen. But I planned to revel in this feeling for as long as I possibly could. With a world of possibility between us.

6

SAVANNAH
PRESENT

A cloud of dust erupted out of a box. I fell over backward to escape it as I coughed violently.

My eyes burned as I straightened to a sitting position and stared at the pile of dusty boxes my mother had recommended I go through while I was here. I'd agreed because I hadn't thought that I'd really left anything here after high school and college. Apparently, I'd been wrong. There were several large boxes full of my stuff. Too much to get through before I met Amelia for lunch.

I peered into the first box and found it full of old clothes. I removed my favorite pair of low-rise jeans with dismay. God, I hoped these never came back in style.

Well, most of this would have to be donated. It was a decade out of style. And even if I could get my ass into those jeans again, I wasn't planning to wear them. I'd be damned if I had to go back to showing off eight inches of torso in a crop top.

I closed the dusty box back up and eased back onto my hands. My eyes scanned the half-full attic. I'd had no idea that my mother was a pack rat. She didn't seem to throw anything away.

I hopped to my feet and walked over to my high school bedroom set. I ran a finger through the dust on the white four-poster. She'd clearly just moved it upstairs. There were four or five wildly out-of-date *full* bedroom sets that I picked out based on the headboards and the various mattresses.

The rocking chair that used to sit on the back porch for ages was up here. I moved the box that was on top of it to the floor, picked up the book underneath it, and sank into the chair, letting it lull me.

This was one of the few possessions that I'd coveted from my mother. It had belonged to her mother, and she hadn't let her husband, Edward, get rid of it when they moved in together. I didn't know what it was doing up here if she had fought so hard for it in the '80s.

I glanced down at the small book in my hand. I flipped it over to look at the cover, but the dark blue leather binding revealed nothing. I cracked it open to the first page and stopped my rocking. The front page read *Diary of Rebecca Charlotte Turner*.

Turner.

That was my mother's maiden name. Before she'd taken Edward's last name of Montgomery. I'd gotten Reynolds from my dad. How old was this diary? Thirty years old?

The pages were yellowing from disuse and likely all the dust collected in the attic. I glanced at the door once and then turned to the first page. *June 7, 1988* was scrawled in my mother's neat hand. I skimmed the page.

It was a rambling count of the beginning of her summer vacation and how her parents had brought her to Savannah the summer before she was to attend the University of Georgia. They barely had enough money to afford a room for the three of them for the summer, and she was miserable.

I gulped. That was the summer she'd met my dad. I only knew that because I'd begged Dad to tell me what happened, thinking the whole thing must have been so romantic at one point. I'd been young and dumb. He'd said they met the summer before college and my mother was pregnant by the new year. That was all he'd say about it after that.

I turned to the next page, and there was my dad's name—Charles. Well, she called him Charlie. Ew.

"Josephine," my mother called as she stomped up the attic stairs.

I snapped the diary closed. I probably wasn't supposed to be reading this.

"How's it going up there?"

"Uh, slow."

My mother appeared in a ruffled baby-pink dress. Her hair was big and her makeup heavy. It was over the top, but it was so her.

"I actually found your diary."

"Oh, that old thing," she said, waving her hand. "I wondered where that had gotten to."

I held it out to her. "I read the first page before realizing what it was."

"You can read the whole thing if you can get through

my teenage angst." Her laugh was a tinkle. "There's nothing in there that I have to hide."

"Really? I can read it?" I asked in disbelief. I couldn't imagine handing over my deepest thoughts to anyone.

"When you get older, you'll realize you don't care what anyone thinks about you anymore. I had to learn that at a young age. It's what's kept me going all these years."

"I've had to learn that lesson too."

I remembered all the things that had cut into me while working on *Academy*—my two failed marriages and all the drama over the years. I'd wanted so desperately to be taken seriously, to matter. But I'd had to give up so much of myself to reach for that, and it hadn't gotten me anywhere.

"Well, I'm off for tea with Nancy. You're welcome to join."

"I'm actually going to see Amelia for lunch."

"Amelia Ballentine?" she asked in surprise. I nodded. "She's lovely. Her little boutique on Broughton is taking off."

"I'm excited to see it. I need a dress for tonight."

My mother waggled her fingers at me. "Off I go. Enjoy your lunch."

I shook my head as she sauntered back down the stairs. We'd never gotten along, but she sure had style.

I wiped off the dust on my thighs as I got up out of the rocking chair. The diary felt heavy in my hand for such a little thing. Maybe it would finally give me answers to all the questions I had about my mother. She'd said that she had nothing to hide, but I still didn't understand why she'd left my dad and married Edward. Why she'd abandoned me so easily but insisted I come here every summer. Why she claimed to love me but could throw me away so easily.

One key point in scriptwriting was understanding character motivations. As an actress, I frequently sought out the scriptwriter to discuss the character with them and get to the heart of *who* the person really was. Maybe this diary would give me a kernel of insight into who my *mother* was. Because everything I knew about her was clouded with what she'd done to me.

Or it might just show me that she had always been the same person.

I sighed and headed back downstairs. I wasn't optimistic, but I was curious.

Ballentine was the chicest boutique in downtown Savannah. Amelia's clothing store was doing so well that she'd bought out the store next door and expanded to fill both spaces. The clothes were fashionable without breaking the bank. Already, the store was full of young girls browsing the wares.

The owner stood by the cash register in sleek white cigarette pants and a ruffled baby-blue top. Her dark hair grazed her waist, and she sipped a sweet tea. Her eyes widened when she saw me walk inside, and she shot me a pageant-queen wave.

The cashier looked up and saw me and gaped. "Is that Josephine Reynolds?" she whisper-shouted at Amelia.

Amelia laughed as I approached and drew me into a quick hug. "Yes, this is Josie."

"Hey, Amelia."

"I heard that *Academy* was shooting in town, but wow," the young girl said with wide eyes. "You're *Josephine Reynolds*."

I grinned at her and sank into my hip. "That's right. Want a selfie?"

Her eyes shot to Amelia. "Would that be okay, Amelia?"

"Go for it."

I snapped a quick shot with the girl and then followed Amelia away from the cash register. I loved my fans even if it was still surreal that I had this rabid of a following, even a decade later.

"You're the talk of the town," Amelia said.

"What else is new?"

She chuckled. "True, true. I'm glad you're back, whatever the reason."

Amelia had been two years younger than us in school. So, we hadn't become friends until after graduation. I'd been working on *Academy* for a few years, and she'd recently graduated from Parsons with a fashion degree. She was working with a designer in New York City and dressed me for more than one red carpet event. I'd been surprised when she left New York to open a boutique in her hometown, but she always just shrugged and said the South owned her heart. I suspected there was more to it.

"Not to be a fangirl," Amelia said, "but ..."

"You want to meet Martin?"

Amelia blushed. "Look, I've been obsessed with Martin Harper since he was on the Disney Channel."

"Yeah. Most girls our age were."

"Is it weird? I don't want it to be weird. I know he's your ex."

"It's not weird. I don't have any feelings about Martin anymore. Plus, I would never come between him and his mega fan, who papered her walls with his magazine pictures."

Amelia laughed. "Oh my God, I cannot believe I told you that once."

"It lives rent-free in my head," I said with a laugh. "And yes, come out with us tonight. Maddox and I are taking the cast to Dub's on River Street."

Amelia's eyebrows shot up. "Maddox Nelson?"

"The one and only."

"What is he doing with the cast?"

"He's actually running the visual effects."

Amelia shot me a suspicious look. "On *your* movie?"

"Trust me, I was as surprised as you are."

Amelia knew precisely what had gone down with me and Maddox over the years. "Well, the party sounds fun."

"Agreed. So, lunch?"

"Yes."

We headed toward the front of the store when the door swung inward. I stalled at the appearance of James Asheford Talmadge IV in a navy suit, crisp button-up, and dark tie. His hair was slicked back, and those blue eyes were bright and intent on Amelia's face.

The last time I'd seen Ash, he'd been a fucking mess. After Lila, he'd dissolved into an alcoholic, fucking anything with legs and being an entitled asshole. But he didn't look like that at all. Two years could really change a man.

"Hey," he said with a genuine smile. "Clary's?"

Amelia's smile dropped as she glanced at me. "Crap. I forgot to mention that I was doing lunch with Josie. You could come with us."

Ash slowly turned to see me standing there. I straightened my spine and smiled at him, shooting him a little wave.

"*James,*" I crooned.

He ground his teeth together. "Josephine."

Ash and I had never really gotten along. Not after what he'd done to Lila at prom. I held grudges, and no matter how we'd tried to put the past behind us for her sake, it had never quite worked. And well, after what had happened at the church two years ago, I was maybe only second in line for the last person he wanted to see again.

"Y'all," Amelia said softly. "Come on."

Ash's smile returned when he looked at Amelia. "I'll pass on lunch. Another time."

Then, he was gone as quickly as he'd come.

I swiveled in shock. "Are you *dating* Ash Talmadge?"

Amelia rolled her eyes. "No!"

"Defensive much?"

She huffed and jerked me toward the door. "We're not dating. He's just, as you can imagine, had a rough two years. I've been a friend. We have a standing lunch. Since my brother moved to Atlanta with Marley, he hasn't really had anyone to help him through everything. I've been the stand-in."

"Romantic," I joked.

She smacked my arm. "It is *not* romantic. There is nothing remotely romantic about me and Ash."

"Except that you've always liked him."

"And he always belonged to someone else," Amelia snapped back. Though she certainly didn't deny the allegation. Finally, she sighed and let the tension roll off her shoulders. "If I thought that he liked me just for me and not as a substitute for what he lost, then sure ... I'd date him. But I'm not going to do anything with him until that point."

"That's fair." I tugged her into a hug. "I'm proud of you. That has to be hard."

"You have no idea."

"Well, you can bring him to the cast party tonight if he promises to behave."

Amelia snorted. "Have you met Ash?"

"At least it's guaranteed to be interesting."

"With you and Maddox in the same room as your ex-husband? I think it was already guaranteed."

I cringed. "Yeah. Wish me luck."

"You're going to need it."

And she wasn't wrong.

7

SAVANNAH

PRESENT

Savannah nights were my favorite in the whole world. I'd traveled all over for *Academy*, but nothing compared to my hometown. People thought it was strange that I claimed Savannah when I'd grown up primarily in Atlanta, but as much as I loved the city, Savannah was special. I could feel it in the sea-salt air and the sticky heat. There were no words for it, except *home*.

After circling for street parking for twenty minutes, I gave up and pulled into a lot. The steps down to River Street were as steep as ever in my Louboutins. I stepped onto the cobblestones and headed toward Dub's. It wasn't the nicest place on River Street by a long shot, but I hadn't wanted to do anything fancy. Maddox would never have shown up.

I was nearly there when a shiny blue sports car zipped right up to the entrance of Dub's. Everyone was staring at the expensive car, and out of it stepped Martin Harper in a three-piece suit. Phones were out, snapping pictures of the television star and my ex-husband. If they noticed me, then things were going to get very uncomfortable.

I stepped backward to avoid the crush of excitement. I almost made it to the door when I heard, "Josephine, darling!"

I took a deep breath and turned to find Martin striding through the crowd, right toward me. That was when the breath went out of the crowd. It was one thing to see Martin in a shiny sports car. It was another thing entirely to see him with *me*.

His arms came around my waist, pulling me against him. My arms went around his neck—because what the fuck else was I supposed to do with a dozen cameras in my face? It was like being back in LA. Fuck.

"Hi, Marty," I muttered into his ear.

He laughed. "That ridiculous nickname still, huh?"

"You know it! Come on." I grabbed his sleeve and pulled him into the bar to escape the cameras. "We have our own room in here."

"Excellent. Wouldn't want to make a scene." I shot him a look, and he cracked up. "What? You didn't like the Maserati?"

"You never did know how to keep a low profile."

"Oh, darling, I've missed you."

I chose not to reply to that comment at all.

When I turned around, I came face-to-face with Maddox. My steps faltered when I saw him taking in me and Martin as we walked into Dub's together. Well, shit. This didn't look good.

I plastered on a smile on and strode the remaining few feet forward. "Maddox!"

He arched an eyebrow at my effusive behavior. "Josie."

"You know Martin, right?"

"I don't believe we've met actually," Maddox said.

His face was neutral, but I knew he was silently seething. He was the one who had signed up for this movie. He was going to have to see Martin and me together for the next six weeks. Might as well get this out of the way.

"Martin Harper, meet Maddox Nelson." I introduced them. "Maddox is the genius visual effects guy that Jimmy hired."

"Right on," Martin said, shaking Maddox's hand. "Glad to have you on board."

"Sure," Maddox said. "Should be an interesting experience."

"Working with Josie always is," Martin said. He winked at me. "You still like a French 75?"

I laughed. "In here?"

Martin looked around, as if just realizing that we were in a sports bar. "Touché. I'll see what they have. Maddox?"

Maddox held up a Creature Comforts beer, a local Georgia craft brewery. "I'm good."

Martin headed to the bar.

Maddox took a sip of his beer and cleared his throat. "So, you and Martin ..."

"No!" I said as defensively as Amelia had earlier today. I released the edge from my voice. "That ship has sailed. I ran into him as I was coming inside."

"He seems to think it's more," Maddox observed. He'd always been able to see through other people like that. Even if he preferred not to interact with them.

"We've spoken for five minutes."

"He got a divorce last year."

I shot him a surprised look. "Are you following gossip rags?"

He grimaced. "Nah, I just ... do my research."

I laughed. "You looked into everyone before you got here, didn't you?"

"Made it easier to deal with all of this," he admitted.

It was so Maddox that it made me ache. I'd missed his relentless desire to learn everything he possibly could about things that interested him. How he used those resources to build bigger and better. Everything else would fall to the wayside as he dived deeper and deeper into his projections, surfacing only when necessary for air and to shower and eat and exist outside his thoughts. But also how he used that intellect to survive being an introvert in an extrovert's world. I had no doubt the last year had been better for him than they had been for me.

Martin returned with my drink—a gin and tonic with a slice of lime. And then the rest of the party trickled in. I threw my arms around my favorite co-worker Iris, unable to believe I hadn't seen her in three years. After all that time on *Academy*, having everyone back together felt like a high school reunion. Not that I'd know because I'd never gone to mine.

And then Amelia Ballentine was at the door. She strode in, wearing a silky pink minidress, with Ash Talmadge holding the door for her. He'd changed out of his suit from earlier today and into khakis and a blue button-up. He'd rolled the sleeves up to his elbows. They cut a striking figure.

Maddox took one step to my elbow and hissed, "What the fuck is that?"

"That is Amelia Ballentine."

"Yeah. No shit. Is she dating *Ash*?"

I glanced at him with a shrug. "She says no. That he isn't over Lila."

"Duh. Anyone who has ever been around him and Lila knows that he's *never* gotten over her. They had longer gaps than two years, and he still went back to her."

"I know that." I shrugged. "What can I do about it? Lila is in Atlanta and happy with Cole. She's not going back to Ash. I won't fucking let her. So, he needs to move on, right?"

Maddox snorted. "Does he?"

I caught his eye, and we both laughed for a second. That was something we'd always agreed on at least. Ash Talmadge was hardly either of our favorite person.

"You want to say hi?"

"Fuck no," he said. "I'm going to get another beer."

He headed to the bar as Amelia hurried across the room and pulled me into a hug. Ash followed in her wake, shooting me a wary look but he kept his mouth shut. I could play nice as long as he did.

"Amelia, this is Martin," I said, introducing her to the heartthrob of her teen years.

Martin kissed her hand like a proper gentleman. Ash clenched his jaw.

I patted him on the shoulder. "Good luck with that."

"What do you mean?" he nearly growled.

"Martin's a bigger flirt than I am. I don't know what's going on with you and Amelia, but I'd stick close."

He met my green eyes with a sneer. "I don't need relationship advice."

I clenched my jaw shut to keep from letting any vicious words snake past my lips. We couldn't fight here.

"All right then. Good talk."

His eyes lifted skyward. "Why do you think I'm here anyway?"

"I have no idea."

Ash's gaze was intent on Amelia. "I'm not going to repeat past mistakes," he said low enough for only me to hear.

I nodded, understanding completely. He'd made every mistake with Lila. Amelia was too good for him, if I was honest, but she was a catch. And he knew it.

Well, that was as much of Ash that I could deal with in one day.

I meandered through the room. It felt good to be in a group of people like this. To be able to just hang out and chat. People I hadn't seen in so long. It felt like being me all over again.

Martin stayed glued to my side for most of the night. We'd always been close like this when we were filming. Even after the divorce, when it should have been awkward, it had only fueled the chemistry on-screen. We hadn't even fought when it ended. And now, he was at my elbow like no time had passed at all.

He kept bringing me drinks to, and I'd already had one too many. If I didn't stop, I'd have to get an Uber home and pick up my car in the morning. I was not looking forward to that. But also, I just wanted to get drunk with my friends and pretend like nothing had changed.

Amelia sidled up to me later while I was deep in conversation with Iris about her latest girlfriend. "Hey, do you see Maddox sneaking out?"

My head snapped up, and I followed her line of sight to the entrance of Dub's. Maddox ran a hand back through his short hair and then yanked the door open. A gaggle of girls pushed in before he could escape.

"He didn't say good-bye," I whispered almost to myself.

Amelia gave me a little push. "He was watching you all night. Go after him."

I didn't wait to think about it. I was across the room and out the door the next minute. I scanned the street to see which direction Maddox had gone, but I didn't see him.

"Fuck," I gasped.

I strode out on the sidewalk and stood on my tiptoes to look over the crowds, but there was no sight of him. I hadn't been that far behind him. How had he gotten away so fast?

Then, I looked across the street and to the Savannah River. My stomach flipped. Maddox was leaning his arms against the railing that looked out across the river. He hadn't left. He'd just needed air.

I checked the traffic and skipped across the cobblestone drive. "Hey," I called as I approached him.

Maddox turned around slowly. "Hey you."

"You're escaping the party already?"

He shrugged. "It's not my scene."

"You're part of this movie."

"Sure."

"You don't have to escape the people you'll be working with for the next six weeks."

"Yeah. Figured I'd leave you to your many admirers."

I leaned my hip into the railing. "They're coworkers. Not admirers."

"They're all in love with you."

"We're friends."

He scoffed. "Okay."

"Is this about Martin?"

"I don't want to talk about any of this."

"Okay," I said. I tipped my head backward, letting the breeze off the river blow the long strands of my black hair. "I always think about you when I'm on the River Walk."

Maddox was silent for a second before facing me. "Why is that?"

I gestured down the river. "We had our first kiss right there."

"Yeah. We all know how well that turned out," he said sardonically.

"I thought the kiss was great."

"And then freshman year was exactly like that party inside." He pointed back at the cast party. "You, the toast of the town, and me, ignored in a corner. Same shit, different year."

"Don't put that shit on me." I looked up into his face. "You had as much to do with why it didn't work as I did."

"No one could measure up to Josephine Reynolds," he said, sketching a bow.

"You're being an ass."

I tipped my head up to look into those bottomless eyes. Tension bristled between us. Potent and intoxicating. So close that I could steal the kiss that was within reach.

He smirked and flipped a strand of my hair. "Ah, then you might actually show interest in me."

I shook my head. "Wow. Okay. I'm not the same person I was freshman year."

"And yet everyone you've dated is an asshole."

"So, you want to do this? What about you, Maddox? What about the girls you've dated since me? The mousy, brainless girls that you're *way* too brilliant to have any interest in, but none of them push you. None of them balance you," I spat back at him. He stiffened at my words. But they weren't untrue. "Two can play at this game."

"I don't want to do any of this, but thank you for reminding me why this didn't work."

I grasped his sleeve before he could leave. "I didn't come out here to fight."

"Could have fooled me."

"I just ... I missed you."

His gaze swept down to where my hand still rested on his sleeve. We'd been so good together over the years. So good that I hadn't appreciated it. I wanted some of that back. I felt like a fool, asking for it, but I knew he felt the same. He had to.

His hand clasped my cheek. "Oh, Josie."

"Maddox," I whispered.

His thumb dragged across my bottom lip. And everything in me tugged toward him.

"We're just too different," he told me baldly.

"We don't have to be."

"But we are," he said, removing his hand from my face and leaving me bereft as he left the boardwalk with my heart in his hand.

PART II

8

SCAD

JUNE 5, 2010

"Okay, Josie, you can do this," I said, giving myself the tenth pep talk since I'd decided on this hare-brained idea. "He's going to say yes. That's all that matters. It's too important. You can do it."

I punched in the six-digit code to enter the visual effects computer lab. I'd gotten the code from a friend who minored in graphics. She'd been more than willing to help me out with my scheme. Anything to avoid working with the most obnoxious graphics guy on campus, Tuck Underwood. Anything.

I took a deep breath and then sauntered into the lab as if I belonged there. I'd taken the same drawing classes required of all film majors, but it hadn't gone well freshman year. Art was hardly my forte. It had always been more conceptual for me. And then I'd avoided any of the computer graphics classes like the plague.

My dream was to become a director. We needed more female directors in the world to actually get women correct and not just overly sexualize them for profit.

Which was why Maddox and I never had classes together and rotated in completely different universes at SCAD. I saw him sometimes in passing when I was out for lunch with friends, but we'd dodged each other for the last couple years.

When I found him hunkered over the high-tech lab equipment, my feet stalled. It had been a long time since I'd been able to just look at him. His curls were as unruly as ever, falling forward into his eyes as he stared down at the keyboard, tossing his head sideways to get them out of his way when he looked up at his work. His jeans were black and ripped, and the matching black T-shirt molded to his muscles.

A memory of all our kisses during our freshman year filtered through my mind. Until it had all crashed and burned. The vibrant sunshine girl hadn't ended up with the grumpy guy.

I swallowed. That was what my roommates had said when it completely fell apart. It was basically what Marley had said when I'd confessed to her over summer break. Afer she'd gotten out her 'I told you so' of course. I hated the assessment, but I still wasn't sure if it was untrue.

I cleared my throat when I finished crossing the room. "Hey."

"I'm busy. Give me ten minutes." Maddox didn't even look up when he said it.

I tried again. "Maddox."

"Ten minutes," he blurted out, typing furiously.

"Well, all right then." I dropped into the seat next to him as he worked out his problem.

No one else was in the lab at this hour. Spring session had ended yesterday in the middle of a vicious thunderstorm, and the start of summer session wasn't for two weeks. Everyone was celebrating on Tybee. My roommate had invited me to do just that, but this was more important. I had all summer for the beach.

Finally, ten minutes later, Maddox came up out of his trance. His gaze locked on me, and he startled, rocking his chair backward.

"Hi," I said with a little wave.

"What are *you* doing here?"

"*Why, Josie, it's been so long since we've seen each other. It's good to see you,*" I said sarcastically for him.

He just steadied his chair. "Josie, why are you here?"

"I can't come to see you?"

He shot me a *don't bullshit me* look. Oh, how I'd missed him. "What do you want?"

"Why do you think I want something?"

"Why else would you be here?"

"I can't want to see you?"

He was already shaking his head, saving his work, and closing everything out. "No."

"Okay. Wow," I said, meeting him as he stood.

"If you don't need anything, I'm going to go."

"Wait." I sighed. "I do need help."

"Ah, there it is. And no."

"You don't even know what it's for."

"I know that I don't want to be involved," he said, shouldering his backpack.

"Look, I'm working on my senior film thesis. It's going to premiere at the SCAD Film Festival in October. I've

67

been working on the concept with my advisor all quarter. I have all my positions filled—script, production, art design, actors." I was rambling, but I couldn't stop. "We both decided that I was going to need visual effects, erm ... VFX, too."

Maddox crossed his arms over his chest. "So?"

"And I could use your help."

"Get someone else."

"But you're the best."

He smirked. "Obviously."

"And oh-so modest."

"It's not vanity when it's fact," he said, stomping out of the lab.

I followed after him down the old hallways and out into the Savannah summer heat. It was a beautiful day. Sunny and bright. No one would guess it had stormed all day yesterday.

I grabbed his arm, pulling him to a stop. "Look, everyone else is already teamed up. The only person available is Tuck Underwood."

Maddox groaned. "I fucking hate that guy."

"Yeah. Everyone does. He's harassed every woman in the school, but daddy has big money, and there will never be any consequences. I cannot work with him."

He cringed at my assessment. "Plus, his VFX are shit."

"Maddox, please," I asked, my voice wavering. I hadn't thought it would be easy to convince him, but I hadn't thought it'd be this hard either.

"I'm busy," he said with a sigh. "I have my own thesis project, which I'm doing solo, except for the voice acting."

"I can voice act," I volunteered immediately.

He arched an eyebrow. "You're not an acting major."

"Maddox, come on. You know I'm a good actor. I was in all of my high school theater productions. I've done acting film work here at SCAD. Just because I want to be a director doesn't mean I can't act."

"And I'm working on my girlfriend's project."

Ah.

There it was.

The girlfriend. I was surprised it had taken this long to get to this objection. Amanda Curtis and I didn't get along. We never had. She was in the film school as well as on the producing track. A mousy, small girl who never spoke up in class when it mattered but still complained constantly.

"Well, what's the use of that big brain of yours if you're not working on multiple projects?" I teased.

He rolled his eyes. "Don't try that with me."

"What?"

"Flirting," he growled.

"You're mistaking charisma for flirtation."

He looked over at me, disbelieving. We both knew that he wasn't doing anything of the sort. But flirting with Maddox came naturally, like breathing.

We stopped in the parking lot. The building was three stories tall and home to visual effects, animation, and gaming. It contrasted with the building where the film department was housed in Adler Hall off River Street. I'd gotten used to stepping out every day to the Savannah River.

My BMW was parked next to the pickup truck he'd had since high school. We'd been the only two cars in the parking lot when I got here. A third one was parked next to Maddox's now.

I turned back around to try to work on convincing him, but his gaze was still on that car.

"Friend of yours?"

"Fuck," he muttered under his breath.

And then we both found Amanda Curtis walking in our direction, looking pissed.

Fuck was right.

"Amanda," Maddox said.

He took a clear step away from me as he went over to his girlfriend. Her blonde hair was cut short in a nondescript bob. Her clothes were plain—jeans, a pastel T-shirt, and Keds.

"Hey, I brought you lunch," she said, holding up a bag from a local bagel shop. "Thought you might be working hard, like normal."

"I was," he said.

"With Josie?"

"Hey, Amanda," I said with a bright smile.

"We weren't working together," Maddox said quickly.

"Maddox is helping me with my senior thesis film."

Amanda's eyes turned as big as saucers. "You are?"

"No!" he said hastily. "No, I'm not."

"It's that or work with Tuck Underwood, and we all know how that would work out."

Amanda grimaced. "Tuck is a creep."

"Right. Exactly. Maddox is a much better option."

Maddox groaned. "Are you going to bother me until I say yes?"

"Yes," I said definitively.

Let him save face in front of his girlfriend. I wasn't here to be a homewrecker. As much as Maddox and I had history, I wasn't that kind of girl.

"Fine," he grumbled. "Send me what you have, and I'll look at it."

"Thank you. Thank you. Thank you!" I said, jumping in excitement.

Amanda crossed her arms. "You'll still have time for my stuff?"

"Of course," Maddox said gently.

"Oh, and I'll do any voice acting you need, Maddox."

"She's voice acting for your film?" Amanda asked, aghast.

"Just if he needs help," I said quickly. "Anyway, I'm going to get out of your hair now. I'll text you. Bye. Thanks again."

I made a hasty retreat. I could already see that Amanda was going to give him an earful. But, well ... I didn't have to work with Tuck Underwood. I got to work with Maddox instead. And that was a fair trade in my book.

9

SCAD

JULY 31, 2010,

"And to your left, you'll find the famous Cathedral of St. John the Baptist," a ghost tour guide began. "It has the highest twin steeples in all of Savannah and is home to the all-boys school, Holy Cross, and the girls school, St. Catherine's."

I skipped around the crowd in Lafayette Square, on my way to my favorite coffee shop in town that overlooked the famed cathedral. I was ten minutes late already. Maddox was going to kill me. I was shocked that I didn't have a bunch of texts, asking where I was. He was perpetually early, and I was always late.

It was hot and overcast, and I hadn't been able to find any parking on the streets. I'd had to park a half-mile away and hoof it in my heels. He'd just have to deal.

I cracked open the door to the coffee shop, craning my neck to look through the small crowd. It wasn't that big. His curls and height should have been easily visible in the modern white space.

But there was no Maddox.

I pulled out my phone and scanned my messages. Nothing from Maddox. I shot him a text.

Did you forget our meeting? I'm here already. I'll order you a coffee.

Despite Amanda's displeasure with Maddox and me working together, it had been nothing but professional all summer. She had even hung out with us at Tybee when Marley and Lila were in town. Nothing out of the normal.

I'd gone into the studio to test out some voices for the animated short film he was drawing, designing, storyboarding, and bringing to life, all on his own. He hadn't lied when he said that all he needed was voice actors. From what I'd seen, it was beyond brilliant. And I couldn't thank him enough for his genius mind on my project. Something was not fitting together, and I needed to get it all in place before we could start filming next month.

I ordered both of our coffees and waited at our usual meeting table, looking out at the cathedral. I shot him another text, letting him know where I was sitting. Then returned my dad's missed call.

"Hey, Josie. Hope you're not busy."

"Just waiting on someone for a meeting. What's up?"

I took a deep breath and prepared myself for the conversation. My dad had fallen on hard times ever since I'd gone off to college. Mom wasn't supporting him anymore since I didn't live there, and the art business was in the gutter. He'd taken a job at an insurance company to get by, and I hated it for him.

"Had a long day, and I'm missing you. I think I'm going to quit."

"Not again, Dad." It was his third job in the last couple months. "I really thought the insurance company was working out."

"How do people live like this? I was thinking of applying to one of those paint pottery shops. There's a new one in Alpharetta."

"Okay, Dad," I said with a sigh. I'd had to ask my mother for extra money last month to help Dad make rent. It was a total clusterfuck and making my life a living hell. I wanted him to get his shit together, but I knew it was so hard for him to do anything but what he loved. Just ... what he loved didn't pay the bills. "If you need money—"

"No," he said quickly. "I don't want you to have to ask your mom again. Just calling to chat."

"Yeah. Okay. I have to get to my meeting."

We said our good-byes, and I hung up with a sigh. God, I couldn't wait for Maddox to get here, so I didn't have to think about it anymore. Where was he?

As I went through my other text messages, another one came in:

Guess what, babe?

My toes curled at the message. His name was Isaiah, and he was an officer in the Army. We'd met on River

Street last weekend when I was sloshed, and we were supposed to go out tonight.

What's that?

I got us Pink House reservations.

My heart stuttered. The Olde Pink House was my favorite restaurant in town. It was hard to get reservations there and ridiculously expensive.

I love that place! Can't wait. See you tonight. xo

Isaiah kept up a steady stream of texts while I waited for Maddox. But there was no response, and after thirty minutes, my coffee was drained, and Maddox was a no-show.

For anyone else, I would have sent off a series of angry messages and blown them off. I needed to go home and get ready for my date. I was meeting Isaiah in a matter of hours, and I still needed to shave and blow out my hair. But Maddox was different.

Maddox didn't miss meetings. He didn't ignore text messages. He never played games or was anything but eternally professional.

I chewed on my lip in worry. Something must have happened. I shot out another text, asking if he was okay, but he didn't respond to that. With a huff, I tossed his cold coffee and hustled back to my car. I was across town and at his apartment fifteen minutes later, stalking up the front steps and banging on the front door.

"Maddox Nelson, are you alive in there?"

There was no answer. His truck was in the parking lot. So, he had to be here. If he and Amanda went somewhere, they always took his truck. She never drove anywhere if she didn't have to. I still found her insufferable to be around, but I'd managed to grin and bear it all summer.

I knocked again. "Maddox?"

When there was still no answer, I tried the knob. And to my surprise, it turned. I slowly crept the door open and peeked my head inside. "Hello?"

"Go away," Maddox grumbled.

He was seated on the floor in front of the coffee table with an assortment of alcohol scattered on the table. My eyes widened in alarm. I'd known Maddox my whole life, and I'd never seen him drink more than one beer in a single night. He always said that he didn't like how out of control he felt when he drank too much. Like it dimmed his genius. Well, he hadn't said that last part, but that was what I thought.

"What are you doing?" I gasped, striding into the apartment.

He lifted a half-empty bottle of tequila in my direction. "What are you doing here?"

"You missed our meeting, Maddox. Remember? Coffee and planning at four o'clock." I tapped my watch. "It's four forty-five now. I have a date at seven. What the hell is going on?"

"Go on your date, Jos," he said, slurring his words. "I'm fine."

I slammed the door shut hard enough to rattle the walls. "You are not fine. You're drinking tequila *straight*."

"Tastes like Kool-Aid."

I grimaced. "How much of that have you had?"

He held up the bottle. "It was full when I started. I think."

"Jesus Christ."

He staggered to his feet, stumbling into the table and barely catching himself. The bottle slipped out of his hand and landed on the ground. Tequila puddled on the carpet.

"Fuck, Maddox." I scurried forward on my heels and grabbed the bottle off the ground.

He took it out of my hand and did another shot. "Thanks."

I yanked it back from him. "Stop. Just stop for a minute."

He chuckled. "All those times you wanted me to get wasted, and now, you're mad that I am."

"This isn't you." He reached for the bottle again, but I held it away from him. "Sit. Let me get you some water. You're going to be sick."

His hands came around my waist, pulling me toward him. I was so startled that I didn't even stop him. "That's not what I want to do with you here."

I opened and closed my mouth in shock. "Maddox ... you're drunk."

"So?"

I carefully extracted myself. "And you have a girlfriend."

"Nope," he said as he staggered backward and

collapsed on the couch. He reached for one of the empty beer cans. "Not anymore."

My face softened. "What happened?"

He shrugged. "We got into a fight. I broke it off."

"I'm sorry."

He snorted. "Are you?"

"Of course, Maddox. My feelings about Amanda aside, you seemed happy."

"She was paranoid."

I headed to the kitchen, deposited the bottle, and poured him a large glass of water. "Paranoid how?"

Maddox followed me into the kitchen and grabbed the tequila bottle. I sighed heavily.

"She thought we were hooking up."

I nearly choked. "What? Why?"

"Because we'd dated before."

"I didn't even flirt with you in her presence," I said as I passed him the water.

He shot me a disbelieving look. "Do you even know what flirting is, Josie? All you do is flirt with everyone."

"Then, she shouldn't take it personal," I argued. But guilt crept into my stomach. I'd thought I was doing a good job of staying away from him, except for work.

"It's you," he said, guzzling half the water before setting it back down. "She wasn't being logical about it."

"So, she broke up with you because of me?" I asked softly.

He shook his head. "Nope. I broke up with her because I was tired of fucking fighting with her about it. I did nothing wrong. I didn't deserve to be treated that way when we were only working together. She has trust issues because her last boyfriend cheated on her."

"Been there."

He took another long swig from the bottle before offering it to me. "Drink with me?"

I checked my watch again. Fuck. I had that date with Isaiah. I'd been looking forward to it, and he had a reservation. But Maddox clearly needed me here. He was a fucking mess, and if I left him, he'd drink himself into a stupor.

I snatched the bottle back from him but didn't take a drink.

He laughed. "Never could resist a good party."

"Better get some music going if this is a party."

He stumbled headfirst to his computer and turned on some horrendous music. I knew he wasn't far from blacking out. Maddox needed me more than my date. I'd just reschedule.

With a sigh, I shot a text to Isaiah.

I'm so sorry. I'm going to have to reschedule tonight. My friend is going through a huge breakup, and they need me.

His response was almost immediate.

What the fuck? We've had this planned all week. If you wanted a reason to cancel, just fucking say so. You don't have to be a bitch.

I stared at his response in blatant alarm. My mouth hung

open in shock. Wow. This guy had been so incredibly sweet all week. Responding to all of my messages with emojis and love-bombing me with sweet nothings. One reschedule, and the real guy came out. He sent a string of texts, calling me all sorts of terrible names. The responses growing more and more terrifying. Within a few minutes, I had to block his number. Good riddance. I dodged a bullet with that one.

"What?" Maddox asked as he came back over to where I was standing. He couldn't even focus on my face. He looked like he was spinning.

"Just canceled my date. The guy was a jerk."

"You deserve someone better," Maddox said.

"Thanks. How are you doing?" I kicked off my heels and went for the water. "Drink more of this water."

"I'm fine. Just come dance with me."

"Dance?" I asked with a laugh. "Since when do you dance?"

"Always." He paused and thought about it. "Or never."

But he grabbed my hand, and we danced around his apartment. He was wasted and clearly grieving his relationship. I felt bad that it had fallen apart because of me. Or at least because of Amanda's own insecurities about me. But I couldn't deny that I was having fun with Maddox like this.

We moved in time to the music. It felt ridiculous, and I couldn't stop laughing. This was probably a better time than I would have had with that jerk anyway.

Maddox grabbed my hand and swung me back into him. We collided with a soft *oof*, and he pulled me tight against him. His words were soft when they left his mouth. "Amanda was right." I tried to pull back to look at his face in question, but he wouldn't let me go. "I am still in love with you."

My eyes closed in pain at the words. At the wasted years. And the fact that only breaking up with his girl-friend had gotten him to admit it to me. Not that he was in any condition to do anything about it.

"Maddox."

But he crashed down on the couch and looked at me with glazed eyes. A few minutes later, he was passed out.

I ran a hand down my face. What a mess.

I rummaged through his clothes and changed into a pair of basketball shorts that I rolled up three or four times and an oversize T-shirt.

When his roommate, Andrew, showed back up around ten, he looked between us with a smirk on his face. "About time."

I snorted. "He and Amanda broke up. I didn't think he should get drunk alone. Can you help me carry him to his bed?"

Andrew nodded, and together, we got him into his bed. I never would have been able to do it on my own. Even with Andrew, I'd barely been much help.

"Thanks."

"Anytime. And, Josie," he said before he left Maddox's room.

"Yeah?"

"I was always rooting for y'all."

I laughed. "Uh, thanks."

He tipped his head at me and then disappeared.

I should probably go home. Maddox would wake up, hungover, and he'd deal with all of that on his own. I could call to check on him. But I found that I didn't want to go home. I wanted to sit here in his bed and watch the easy rise and fall of his chest. To see that he was safe.

I tucked my legs under the covers and turned on my side to watch him sleep. I brushed a strand of his curls off his forehead. It immediately flopped back down into place. But he reached out for me, finding my hand and pulling it against his chest, as if I belonged there, as if I were precious.

So, I lay there with my hand against his chest until I succumbed to sleep.

10

SCAD

AUGUST 1, 2010

When I woke, there was a body pressed against my back with a strong arm around my waist. My eyes fluttered open as I returned to consciousness with alarm. I rolled over in bed and found Maddox still fast asleep.

My body relaxed back into the bed as the night before returned to me. I'd momentarily forgotten that I'd fallen asleep in his room. The fact that he was still asleep was a good thing. I could probably slip out before he ever found out that I'd spent the night.

Except when I tried to move out of the bed, his arm tightened around my waist and dragged me back into place. I laughed softly. So much for that plan. Even hungover and asleep, Maddox didn't want me to go.

I nudged his shoulder lightly, and his eyes blinked lazily open. Then, he saw me lying in bed with him.

"Oh fuck," he ground out, jerking backward. He clearly regretted that decision because he groaned and leaned forward, hands to his head. "Fuck. How much did I drink?"

"Three-quarters of a bottle of tequila and at least a half-dozen beers. Before that, I'm not sure."

"You're ... in my bed," he said slowly.

"Yeah. When you missed our meeting, I came over to check on you, and you told me about Amanda."

"I missed our meeting? Shit. Sorry."

"It's okay."

"Did we, uh ..." He gestured to the bed.

"Sleep together?" I shook my head. "No. You were obliterated before I even got here. I stayed to make sure you didn't die in your sleep."

"Uh ... thanks."

"Tequila Maddox was a good time though," I said with a teasing grin. "You've been holding out on me."

He groaned again. His cheeks flamed. "What did I do?"

"You insisted that we were having a party, we danced to ridiculous music, and, well ... you confessed that you still loved me."

Maddox winced. "I did?"

"Yeah, but it's no big deal," I said quickly for his benefit. "I know you were just drunk."

"Yeah. I was ... really drunk."

"We all say and do stupid shit when we're drunk."

"This is why I never drink at parties. Fuck."

"Well, I stayed to make sure you were okay. I've never seen you like that before."

"I don't think I've ever been that drunk before."

I laughed. "I have. And I know how you must be feeling. Go take a shower, drink some water, and grab a few Tylenol. I'm going to make breakfast."

"You're going to make breakfast?" he asked in confusion.

"I don't think you can stomach more than eggs and toast, right?"

His hand went to his stomach as it gurgled. "Oh God, the thought of food makes me sick."

I tried to hide my laugh. "As I thought. I know how to take care of drunk people. Take your time."

I scurried out of bed as quickly as I could and padded out to the kitchen. I hadn't been able to take the look of discomfort on his face. As if admitting how he'd felt about me had broken some code. I'd pretend that it had all been a stupid, drunk joke if he wanted. That was fine. Easier even.

A half hour later, Maddox walked into the kitchen, his curls still wet. There were thumbprint bruises under his eyes, but he looked better than when he'd first woken up. He dropped into a seat at the kitchen table, and I set a plate of eggs in front of him.

"Thanks for this."

"No problem."

He took one bite and groaned. "These taste like Gran's."

"Well, that's a compliment if I've ever heard one." Gran was the best cook I'd ever met.

He shoveled more eggs into his mouth, and I shook my head.

"Take it easy. You don't want to get sick."

He slowed, but the eggs were decimated in a matter of

minutes regardless. "Did you say that you had a date? Or did I make that up?"

"Oh," I said softly. "Uh, yeah. I canceled."

"Fuck, Jos, I'm sorry. You didn't have to do that."

"The guy was an asshole after I did it and called me a bitch."

"What?" he asked in shock. "For *canceling*?"

"Rescheduling even."

"What a dick."

I shrugged and pushed my eggs around my plate. "I blocked his number. It was for the best, I guess."

Maddox took a long sip of his water before responding again. "I really appreciate you taking care of me last night."

"Of course. Anytime."

"But, uh …" He looked down at his plate and then up at me tentatively. "I didn't lie when I was drunk."

I met his gaze. Those dark eyes trying to say everything he couldn't now that he was sober.

"I know," I whispered.

"You do?"

"Yeah. I mean, I assumed at least."

"And you …" he began. "How do you feel?"

"I canceled my date and stayed the night to make sure you didn't die," I told him bluntly.

"Go out with me."

I blinked in surprise. "What? You broke up with Amanda *yesterday* and then got so fucking wasted."

"I know that. None of it changes how I feel about you."

"It didn't work freshman year. I'm still a party girl, and you're still the introvert."

"Who cares?" he said with the first hint of a smile. "It's one date. If you hate it, then we can go back to being professional."

He said that as if it were a real possibility. But Maddox Nelson had been in love with me since we had been kids. One date would change everything. It was dangerous, especially considering how it had all fallen apart freshman year, just like Marley had warned me. But I couldn't deny that I wanted him. I'd always wanted him despite our differences.

"You know it'd never be that easy."

He reached across the table and took my hand, drawing circles on my palm. "And I want to try anyway. Jump with me, Josie."

So, I jumped.

11

SAVANNAH
PRESENT

Two weeks into filming *Academy*, and everything was rolling smoothly. I was used to the long days. At first, I'd missed them, and now, it just felt like work again. Amazing work that I desperately wanted to be doing, but work nonetheless.

When I wasn't needed on set, I'd lounge in my trailer and pull out my mother's book. It was taking me forever to get through. Not because it wasn't interesting, but because I had to come up for air a lot. My mother sounded like ... me.

In the first quarter of the book, it was page after page about how she'd met my dad and she was so in love. Even some sexy passages that I would have rather gouged my eyes out than read, but here we were. There was a brief mention of my mother's husband, Edward. It was more of an after thought than anything. Just something that said he was one of my dad's friends, which I'd never known. Nor had I known that they'd both been Holy Cross boys.

I yawned and turned to the next page. My fingers

stilled on the page. Well, well, well, Edward Montgomery had officially made his appearance. I skimmed the next two pages. All about how my dad had gone out of town on a family vacation to Florida and my mom spent the week with Edward while bored. Except it was clear, at least from my estimation, that Edward was both in love with her and jealous that his best friend had gotten there first.

My eyebrows rose, and I closed the book. Maybe I'd finish those salacious details later.

I pulled out my phone as I popped a gummy bear in my mouth and shot a text to my dad. I'd told him last week that I was reading my mother's journal. He'd told me to take it all with a grain of salt—it was my mother, so obviously. But he'd never told me Edward was his best friend.

Excuse me, sir! Edward was your best friend?

I could practically hear my dad sighing as he read the message.

That didn't seem relevant.

Pretty relevant. Mom married your best friend! What the fuck?

Maybe you don't need to read that journal after all.

Mom said she had nothing to hide.

The past is in the past, Jos. I love you, but I've left it where it belongs. So should you, and so should your mother.

Fine. Fine.

I love you too.

I took a sip of water. Neither my mom nor my dad ever talked about what had gone down. It was kind of nice to get details about it, but maybe I should leave my dad out of it. It sounded like he had gotten the short end of the stick. I didn't want to hurt him by bringing it up.

I reached for the journal again to keep reading just as my computer started ringing. I pressed to answer the incoming video chat. Marley's face appeared on the screen.

"Josie!" she said cheerfully, her dark curls bouncing with excitement.

"Hey, Mars. What's up?"

"I wanted to check in on the movie. My movie-star friend." Mars rolled her eyes. She loved my celebrity status as much as she found it ostentatious. I'd always be the Josie who had crashed in her bedroom on the weekends.

"It's going great. Two weeks in. Four more to go and then reshoots if we need them."

"That's good to hear. Derek and I are going to come into town next weekend for the holiday. He's actually taking Memorial Day off. So, we'll be free."

Derek's face appeared behind her, looking exasperated. "I take time off all the time."

Marley made a face at him. "You're a workaholic."

"Who are you talking to? Pot, meet kettle," he argued.

"Don't argue with my lawyer, Mars," I said with a laugh.

He grinned and gestured to me. "Listen to your friend."

"Arguing with him is the greatest pleasure of my life."

I snorted. Man, she wasn't wrong. And honestly, Derek liked it anyway. He rolled his eyes and went back off the screen.

"Derek wants to sail," Marley continued, unperturbed. "Maybe we can go to the beach."

"*You* want to go to the beach?"

She sighed. "Well, no. I don't want to burn to a crisp, but I know you love it."

"True. Are Lila and Cole coming too?"

"I invited them, but they have Falcons training camp coming up." Marley glanced back at Derek and dropped her voice. "Plus, I think Derek wants to hang with Ash. Probably better to make a separate girls' trip."

"Probably. It's not like we want a Lila-Cole-Ash drama-fest."

"Exactly."

"I have actually *seen* our lovely friend James," I said with a smirk on my lips.

"Oh God, did y'all kill each other?"

"We did not. But"—and it was my turn to lower my voice—"I think he might be seeing Amelia."

"What?" she squawked.

"She claims that they're not, but ..." I shrugged. "You

be the judge. They'll probably come to the beach with us for Memorial Day."

"Well, that should be interesting. I don't know if it will be more fun to warn Derek or to watch him explode when he realizes his best friend is going after his little sister."

"Oh, certainly the latter," I said, and we both burst into giggles.

"So," Marley said, changing the subject, "what do you think of Gran's house? The renovations are amazing, right?"

I bit my lip and leaned back. "Well, uh, about that. I haven't been."

"What? Why not?"

"Maddox and I are ..."

Marley tipped her head back on a sigh. "Again?" she groaned.

"You have no room to talk! You and Derek were the definition of *toxic*!"

She snorted. "Yeah, we were."

Our eyes met, and we said at the same time, "Are."

I couldn't stop laughing. I felt so lucky to have these best friends. I wished that Lila could come in town for Memorial Day too. Navigating her past relationships was a full-time job. And sometimes, I wished we could all go back to when it had been easier.

"Anyway, whatever is going on with you and Maddox, that isn't an excuse. I didn't give him my half of Gran's house and let him renovate our childhood home for him to refuse to show it to anyone."

"Mars, it's fine."

But there was a glint in Marley's eyes that I knew all too well. "It's not. I'll fix this."

The camera flashed black. She'd hung up on me. Oh Lord. This was going to be … interesting.

I flopped back onto the couch, bringing the diary with me. I should probably go find Maddox and apologize for whatever Marley was about to do. But after what had happened with him on River Street, I didn't have it in me.

Fifteen minutes later, a knock sounded on my trailer door.

"Come in," I called.

The door creaked open, and Maddox Nelson stood in the doorway. He was in the black jeans and gray T-shirt he practically wore as a uniform to set. He'd had another haircut since I'd last seen him, taming his dark curls into a semblance of order. It was so short and professional that it made me ache for the wild and unruly youth he'd been.

"Hey."

He nodded his head at me. "Mind if I come in?"

"Sure." I scooted over on the couch and set the diary down on the coffee table.

He stepped into the trailer and pulled the door closed behind him. "So, I have been properly chastened."

I laughed. "What does that mean?"

"Mars called and yelled at me for not showing you Gran's house yet."

"I did not put her up to that."

He held up a hand. "Trust me, I know my sister. No one can tell her what to do."

"That is a categorical fact."

"So ... you could come over if you wanted to see it. Gran sort of raised you too," he said, his voice catching on the word.

"She did. I miss her."

"Yeah. Me too," he said softly.

There was a moment of silence between us at the recognition of the loss. I hadn't been able to be here for Gran's funeral and still regretted it. She had been a miraculous woman.

"But you don't have to show me the house if you don't want to. I know ... we aren't exactly on great terms. And I wouldn't want to impose. It was Marley's idea."

"Do you want to see the house?"

"Well, yeah ..."

"Then, you can see it. It's Gran's house still, and she never knew a stranger. She'd be pissed at me for not offering proper hospitality," he said with a slight smile. "She told me once that nothing was more important than Southern hospitality, except for people who didn't like sweet tea. They didn't deserve it."

I burst into laughter. "God, that sounds just like her."

"She always had those wise phrases that were full of compassion to a point."

"She loved unconditionally."

"And was the best cook."

I smiled. "Her biscuits and gravy. I still dream about them."

"Tell me about it. I cannot get the gravy to thicken like she used to." He ran a hand back through his hair. "And most of her recipes are like, *add a dash of this and a hint of that*. No measurements, all intuition. And it turns out, I have no intuition in the kitchen."

"Oh, Gran."

I personally wanted to see those recipes. I'd always been a pretty good cook. I got good at it when Dad was too engrossed in his current sculpting or pottery project to remember to put dinner together. But for that year of isolation, I'd really invested in my cooking and baking skills. I'd even had a sourdough starter. Yes, even I rolled my eyes at myself.

"So, are you going to come over?" Maddox's dark eyes met mine, and I wasn't sure what to read in them.

Once, he'd been such an open book. I'd known that he loved me forever. Then, something had shifted, and like a dropped glass egg, it'd shattered into a million pieces. Now, I couldn't tell exactly what he wanted.

I thought he'd made himself clear when he told me we were too different. This was going nowhere. Even our friendship was tenuous since it was based entirely on our shared history. A tense and tangled mess of a history.

It was entirely possible he was doing this because Marley had asked him to. But was it wrong for my heart to hope that it meant something more?

When it came to Maddox Nelson, I could only ever hope that we'd jump one more time.

So, I nodded and said, "Okay. Sure. I'll come by after work."

12

SAVANNAH
PRESENT

M y mother wore an extravagant blue cocktail dress and had a martini in her hand. Her bright red lips smiled back at me. "Don't you look lovely?"

I pushed my hands down the front of my purple sundress. It wasn't anything fancy, but I'd picked it up from Amelia's boutique. I clearly had not brought enough summer clothes with me to survive a Savannah summer. "Thanks. You look great too. Where are you going?"

"Oh, there's a charity function at the yacht club." She waved the martini, as if it were nothing. "My gentleman caller is picking me up any minute now."

I raised an eyebrow. "Gentleman caller? You're dating someone?"

"Ah, don't be blasé, Josephine. What else is there to do in this town?"

I laughed. "Well, have fun." I turned to go but stalled and faced her again.

"Yes?"

"Did you love my dad?" I whispered.

My mother didn't even flinch at the question. "Of course I did."

"Okay."

"Why would you ask that?"

"I'm reading your diary, and I don't know ... I'm not that far in, but in the end, you chose Edward."

"I did."

"Why?"

"Finish the diary and then ask me that again."

I nodded at her. My stomach churned. In the diary, she'd been so *happy* with my dad. He'd been at Holy Cross on scholarship. She'd been there for the summer. Her family wasn't exactly poor, but poor by old-money standards. And then Edward came in like a wrecking ball. Had he ruined it all? Could we have been one big, happy family my entire life if it wasn't for him? Or had it always been doomed to end the way it had?

"All right. Have a good night."

"You too, darling," she said as I headed out the front door.

With all the thoughts about my mother's mysterious past crawling through my brain, I went on autopilot over to Gran's. I'd lost count of how many times I'd made that drive in my life. But it was wild to think that it now belonged to Maddox.

I parked behind Maddox's Jeep Wrangler on the street in front of the Spanish moss–covered oak that we'd climbed on as kids, and I looked up at the house. The exterior had been painted because the light-blue Victorian was brighter and the white wraparound porch was more vibrant. As I hopped out of the car and crossed the street, the iconic yellow door called me home.

As I climbed onto the porch, I tried to settle my nerves. I'd been in this house hundreds of times. There was nothing different about today. Nothing at all.

I could lie to myself with the best of them.

With a harsh breath out, I knocked on the front door.

Yapping immediately started on the other side. Clomping sounds followed from the direction of the stairs, and Maddox yelled, "Walt, cut it out!"

The front door was yanked open. Maddox held his shih tzu, Walt, in his arms. His smile widened at the sight of me.

"Wow, you look"—he cleared his throat—"uh, beautiful. You look beautiful."

"Thanks," I muttered. "The dress is new."

"I like it." He averted his gaze and jerked the door open wider. "Come on in."

I stepped into Gran's house, and Maddox set Walt on the ground. He jumped on my legs, demanding attention. I gave him some serious belly rubs before turning back to the house.

It was ... miraculous. Somehow, it looked just as it always had and completely different. The original hardwood floors had been sanded and refinished. They were glossy, as if straight out of a magazine. The walls had a fresh coat of paint. The walls between the kitchen, living, and dining rooms had all come down. So, the space was wide open and inviting.

I gawked as I stepped into Gran's kitchen, which had

always felt too small. "You knocked out the back porch," I gasped.

He laughed softly. "Marley had the same reaction, but a bigger kitchen was a necessity. Plus, I built a new porch out back too."

The kitchen was twice the size it had once been with all the counter space a girl could ask for and had a new industrial-sized refrigerator, double oven, and cupboard space. I practically drooled over all the little touches, including all of Gran's favorite plates and little trinkets that made the more modern space feel like home.

"This is even better than my place in LA. I should have had you design the kitchen, apparently."

He smirked. "It's almost like I have a good spatial reasoning."

"Yeah, yeah. Genius."

I followed him around the rest of the house with Walt leading the way.

"Stay here, you mangy mutt," Maddox said affectionately, tossing Walt a toy. Walt snuggled into a dog bed and chewed on the toy.

"Is that going to work?"

He laughed. "Probably not."

In the master bedroom, he'd ripped up the old carpet and added wainscotting to the ceiling. The room was entirely Maddox. All dark colors and carefully artistic vibes. The bathroom was unrecognizably beautiful.

Walt took the stairs to the second floor ahead of us. Maddox rolled his eyes and then started up them. The stairs had been widened. A concept that I was sure had no idea more difficult than I could imagine.

Marley's bedroom had been converted into a guest bedroom. Gran's bedroom set took up the majority of the space. It had a female touch that I was sure Maddox wouldn't have been able to replicate without Gran's things in his possession.

"And this is now my office," he said, opening the door to his old bedroom.

Walt entered first, collapsing into another dog bed, clearly exhausted from his display of exuberance.

I stepped inside, and my eyes immediately found the Oscars resting on the new built-in bookshelves along the back wall. "Wow," I whispered, walking over to them. "Do you mind?"

He shrugged. "They're just paperweights."

I rolled my eyes. "Only you."

"Isn't your Emmy just a glorified paperweight?"

"It's not quite as pretty as this," I admitted.

Maddox scoffed. "Well, what about your Teen Choice Award?"

I scowled at him. "Don't bring that up."

"What was it again? Best On-Screen Kiss?"

"Best Kiss, thank you very much. Iris and I still have the hottest kiss on television." I set one of his Oscars down with a thunk. I wasn't jealous. I wasn't ... at all. Okay, maybe just a little bit.

"I won't argue with you."

I winked at him. "Oh, I bet."

He leaned back in the doorway and crossed his arms over his chest. "Well, what do you think?"

"You did an amazing job. I was skeptical when I first heard about the renovations, but it's perfect. It's new and still so Gran. From the brass mirror in the entranceway to the little teapot in the kitchen and her bedspread. You did good work."

He nodded, his eyes softening at the compliment. "I'm glad you like it."

"I really do."

"And you? How's it going at your mom's?"

I sighed. "Fine, I guess. She's still the same Rebecca Montgomery, you know?" I took a seat behind his enormous desk, which had a half-dozen monitors on it. "She's at a charity function with her *gentleman caller* tonight."

"Did she say that?" he asked, making a face.

"Yep! Good times. But ..." I chewed on my lip. I hadn't told anyone about the diary, and it honestly felt strange to even think that I was reading it.

"What?"

"I found her diary from when she was young. I didn't realize what it was when I picked it up. She said I could read it."

His eyes widened. "Seriously?"

"Yeah, she said she had nothing to be ashamed of. But it's like a love triangle between my dad and Edward. They were Holy Cross boys."

He blinked twice. "Your *dad* was a Holy Cross boy?"

"On scholarship, like Lila."

"That makes sense. He doesn't strike me as an Ash Talmadge or a Derek Ballentine."

"Obviously not. But Edward Montgomery sure was. And what he wanted was his best friend's girl."

"Your mom?" he guessed, and I nodded. "Oh, what a tangled web we weave."

"I haven't finished it yet, but I'm starting to suspect she told me to read it so that I'd start seeing her as ... a real human being."

"Instead of the terrible mother she was?"

I shrugged. "Yeah. I don't forgive her for the shit I dealt with, growing up, but it's still weird."

"I could see that. I'm glad that I don't have to deal with my mom anymore."

"Yeah. No contact since the court case?"

He snorted. "Yeah, right. If only I were that lucky. But I told her if she came by the house again, I'd file a restraining order. She cussed me out and left. Good riddance."

"I'm sorry, Maddox."

"I'm better without her." He looked around the house he'd restored and how much it would have made Gran and Gramps proud. "I was raised by better people anyway."

"You turned out all right."

"You too," he said sincerely.

I much preferred this version of Maddox. It had always been better when it was just the two of us. When everyone else got involved was when things got difficult. We were friends first and foremost. It was nice to remember that.

"So, uh, Marley mentioned she was coming into town next weekend," Maddox said, toeing the doorframe.

"Yeah. Derek wants to go sailing. I guess Lila isn't coming because of training camp."

"And Ash," Maddox finished for me.

"Yeah. That too."

"So, you're going to go with them?"

"Well, yeah. Are you?"

He nodded. "Not sure I have a choice with Mars."

I laughed. "True. Is it ... is it okay that we're going together?"

"We're here right now, and it seems fine."

"You know what I mean."

His gaze snapped up to mine. The tension that always boiled just under the surface returned. I wanted to crash into him at that look. He'd told me exactly what he thought—that we were too different and could never work—but with that one open window, I could finally see how much of that was false.

He wanted to be around me as much as I wanted to be around him. No matter the time or distance between us, the want was always there. It had always been there. And being around him again in this city made me want it more than ever.

"It's hard to be around you," he admitted.

"It's harder to pretend I don't want to be around you though."

His gaze softened further at my earnest words. "Yeah, I know." He ran a hand back through his hair. "We can't ever just be ... normal, can we?"

"We have history."

"Indeed." He sighed, his eyes moving to where Walt was snoring on the dog bed. He shot him a fond smile. His eyes went distant, as if he were seeing the whole history I'd mentioned. Finally, he nodded. "Okay. I'll hang out next weekend. But ... it doesn't mean anything." He was careful with his words. "We've done this over and over again. I just don't have it in me to crash and burn again."

I gulped. "If that's what you want."

But I knew that we were going to Tybee Island, and Maddox and I had inescapable memories there. He was guarding his heart, but I wanted to show him that he didn't have to this time.

13

SCAD

AUGUST 7, 2010

"You're not going to tell me what we're seeing?" I asked Maddox skeptically.

I'd agreed to this date last week over breakfast. One date, and if it wasn't what I wanted, then we could be professional again. As if that was ever going to be possible. Maddox had insisted on an all-day date. I'd looked at him, exasperated, but when he'd shown up in his truck and driven me out to Tybee Island, how could I argue?

We splashed in the water, lounged in the sand, and sketched. It felt like high school all over again—in the best way. We skipped out before the crowds showed up and went to The Crab Shack for their famous low-country boil. I gorged myself on seafood until I thought I'd be sick. It was all so delicious.

After we returned to his apartment to shower and change out of our beach attire, he told me we were seeing a movie and left it at that. The only thing worth seeing in theaters was *Inception*, and everyone in the film department had already watched that masterpiece. I was sure

Maddox had seen it, considering the visual effects were top of the line.

"Nope. You will just have to be surprised," Maddox said.

But he parked on Broughton, ran around to open my door, and then took my hand as we headed toward Trustees Theater, which was the home of the SCAD Savannah Film Festival. The theater wasn't likely to be showing any mainstream films. It was mostly Oscar-nominated films and indie films that only us film junkies had heard of.

"It doesn't even list a film," I argued.

"I might have called in a favor." He smirked at me, all self-confident. Where had this been his entire life?

A favor. Well, I hadn't expected that. Apparently, he'd taken my words as a challenge. My grumpy, introvert boy was pulling out all the stops.

We stepped inside the theater, which could easily seat a thousand. A couple dozen people were already inside, and we took seats at the center for the best view.

"What have you done?" I whispered as the room darkened.

He passed me a ticket stub. I squinted down at it in the dark, and then my breath left in a whoosh.

"*Casablanca*."

My eyes met his, and he smiled. "Your favorite."

"I've never seen it on a big screen."

"I know."

Tears came to my eyes before I could think better of it, and I swiped at them.

"You're crying," he said with concern lacing his voice. "What's wrong? Are you okay?"

"This is the nicest thing anyone has ever done for me."

"Oh," he whispered. "Well, good."

I laughed through the tears. "Yeah, you did good."

He tugged me forward into a swift kiss. "Also, you can go ahead and recite all the lines to me as they happen."

"What?" I asked. "I'm not that bad!"

"You forget that I've seen this movie with you before."

I huffed, but it was good-natured. "Fine. You asked for it though."

We both laughed until someone behind us shushed us. I smothered my laughter and stared up at the screen. And then I was entranced as my favorite movie played on the big screen. I didn't know how many times I'd seen it, but I never got tired of it. There were a dozen other old films that I considered my favorites, but there was something about *Casablanca*. Something about the wistfulness of the romance, the melancholic ending. I loved it all.

I was crying again by the time the credits rolled.

Maddox and I stayed in our seats while everyone else filed out of the theater. I watched until the reel ended and then sighed.

"I'll never get tired of it."

"It's one of the best of all time for a reason. I wish they still made movies like this."

I laughed. "Nah, they could never do this again today. We've moved forward. We just need to be willing to take chances."

"Are we still talking about film?"

"I don't know. Are we?"

He smirked. "Come on."

He took my hand, and then we were rushing back out of the theater and to his truck. I was barely inside when his hands were on me, sliding me hard across the leather seat. Our mouths collided with a desperation I'd been holding back all day. I'd had fun at the beach. It had been magic to see my favorite movie in a theater. But I'd be a liar if I said I hadn't been thinking about where exactly this night would end.

Despite the incredible kiss right before freshman year and the parties we'd attended and the line we'd toed at the time, we'd never made it all the way. It was as if we were both waiting for the right time, the perfect moment. And then it had never happened. Because moments were what you made of them. I damn well was not wasting this one.

I pushed myself into his lap. My legs came on either side of his, straddling him. A honk came from the steering wheel, and I gasped, ducking my head.

Maddox laughed into my hair and then lifted my head back to look at him. I saw desire swirl in his dark irises right before his lips descended on me again. I settled against his lap. The hem of my skirt pushed up to the top of my thighs, and I could feel exactly what I was doing to him through his shorts.

"Fuck," he groaned as I tugged his bottom lip into my mouth and ground my hips against him.

"Yes, please," I whispered.

His hands came to my hips, forcing me down harder. "Josie, I ..."

"We should get back to your place."

"Are you sure?"

"Do I seem unsure?" I asked as I swiveled my hips hard against his cock.

He smirked. "I suppose not."

I pressed our lips together, devouring him whole. I was so ready to get him home and remove all these unnecessary clothes, and at the same time, I was half-tempted to fuck him right here on Broughton. We might give the line at Leopold's a show.

"Okay, okay, okay," he said as his hands slipped up my skirt. "We should go."

"Yes," I said breathlessly, urging him onward.

A finger skimmed down the center of my lace thong. I moaned and arched into him. He stiffened hard against me.

"Jesus Christ," he muttered. His hands came back to my ass, lifting me off him and setting me down in the seat next to him. "My place isn't far. Buckle up."

I pouted at him as I slid the lap belt over my waist. "I was having fun."

He looked desperate at those words. "Trust me, I was too."

He pulled out of his spot in front of the theater and careened down Broughton toward his place.

"Well, that doesn't mean I can't have any fun."

"What do you ..."

But he trailed off as I reached for his pants, unbuttoning them and sliding down the zipper.

"Josie ..."

I should have waited until we got back to his place.

But that look on his face that said he never in a million years would have done this made me want to do it even more. I'd dated enough guys who would have demanded road head that having one who would never even consider it as an option was ... hot. Who knew that blow jobs could be hot when I *wanted* to give them instead of being coerced into them?

I removed his cock from his boxers. He sucked in a breath as I circled my hand around him.

"Fuck, fuck, fuck."

We came to a red light. He looked anxiously over at the other cars around us, but no one was paying attention. And if they were, they could look elsewhere.

I lowered my mouth onto his cock. The leather steering wheel creaked as he tightened his grip, and then the truck jerked forward as the light changed. I slicked my tongue around the head. He moved his hips upward in response. I smirked and took him fully in my mouth.

His breathing hitched as I bobbed up and down.

"Mmm," I moaned as I worked him with my hand, paying close attention to the head.

I licked pre-come off the tip, tasting the saltiness of him on my tongue.

"Fucking hell, Josie."

By the time he pulled into the parking lot of his apartment, I could tell he was close. He released the steering wheel, burying his hands in my hair.

He worked his hips upward as I felt him giving in to the feeling. He'd had to hold back as he drove. His mind only half on the task at hand. But now, he was all mine.

And just as I deep-throated him, he made a sharp grunt and then came in my mouth.

"Oh fucking hell," he groaned as he finished.

I swallowed him down and sat back on my seat. "Hot," I muttered.

He blinked at me. "Me? That was the single hottest fucking thing that has ever happened to me."

I grinned like a Cheshire cat. "You held out a long time."

"I didn't trust myself to have an orgasm while *driving*."

I laughed. "Fair."

He righted himself in a slight daze, and then we headed upstairs to his apartment. The apartment had been cleaned since I'd been here last weekend. His room-mate, Andrew, was nowhere to be seen. Maddox must have suggested he clear out.

"Do you want a drink?" he asked after closing the door.

I shook my head. "That's not at all what I want."

Maddox's arm slung around my waist. He tugged me backward and pushed me hard against the front door. "And what is that?"

My eyes were wide. "What do you think?"

"Should I return the favor?"

"I don't think it was a favor," I said with a smirk.

His hand slipped under my skirt and found the outline of my thong. "You want me to make you come?"

I bit my lip. "Where exactly did my introvert go?"

He arched an eyebrow. "It's just me and you, Jos. I have no reason to hold back."

My body softened at those words. "What did you have in mind?"

Maddox grinned devilishly and then dropped to his knees before me. I squeaked as he dragged my thong down my legs, tossing it behind him casually. Then, he lifted my leg up over his shoulder and buried his face in my pussy.

"Oh!" I gasped, dropping one hand in his hair.

He dragged his tongue up the slit of my pussy lips to the apex of my thighs, circling it roughly around my clit. I saw stars at that. I had already been wet and undeniably turned on from the road head. And his groan must have been him realizing it.

He met my gaze. "Someone liked giving head."

I whimpered, following the track of his hand up my inner thigh. Two fingers opened me to him, and then he slipped them home. I tipped my head back. Fucking fuck. My walls were already contracting around him, begging for more, more, more.

Then, his tongue was against my clit again as he dipped those two fingers in and out, in and out. My legs trembled from the effort of holding myself up as he ate me out. I could make myself come in a matter of minutes with my fingers wet against my clit. But guys, they didn't usually quite get the tempo.

Maddox was in another league. His tongue was perfect parts demanding and coaxing. Like I was on a runaway train that only he knew how to stop from falling off the cliff.

And then I did fall, coming against his mouth with a shout. My head hit the back of the door with a thunk. I saw stars and nearly collapsed forward over him as everything shattered inside of me.

He looked up at me with a grin, and then he slowly rose to his feet and drew me tight against him. "See how good you taste."

Then, his lips were on mine, and I could taste my arousal. I shivered at the intimacy of it. Of how *hot* it was.

His hands came back to my ass, lifting me effortlessly into the air. I swung my legs around his hips and let him carry me into his bedroom. He slammed the door behind us. Together, we crashed onto the bed.

I'd slept here last weekend, never knowing that we'd end up right back in this bed for all different reasons.

Maddox stripped quickly out of his clothes, and I followed close behind. As if we couldn't get naked fast enough. This had been building for years. I'd thought it would happen three years ago. But I couldn't deny that this felt like the right time. Like all those other moments had been building up to this.

His lips were on mine again. His hands ran down my sides. Our bodies pressed tight together.

"I should get a condom," he groaned.

"I'm on birth control."

"Good," he said and then fished in his side table.

I tugged the condom out of his hand, ripped it open, and slid it down the length of him. His eyes tracked me the whole time. No words needed to be said. We both wanted this. We'd both wanted it for a long time.

As he laid me out on the bed before him, bringing my leg up to his hip, everything slowed. The shape of his beautiful lips. The tilt of one side as he looked down at me admiringly. The intensity in his gaze that said everything neither of us had ever uttered.

I reached a hand up to his cheek and drew his lips to mine. "Please," I murmured against them. "Please, Maddox, I'm yours."

He tilted his forehead against mine as he slid inside of me. We both gasped in our mingled breath. Then, he was seated fully in my pussy, and everything that had tightened in my core loosened.

"Oh," I whispered on a sigh. "Yes."

"Yes," he repeated.

He slid his arms around my back, and I tugged him closer, closer, closer. Until not a millimeter of space was left. And then we moved. A build that started as a slow pace until it turned feverish. Still, we held tight to one another. I'd never had sex like this. Never felt like I was going to be thrown loose in the abyss if I let him go. But it was more passionate and irrevocable than any other moment in my entire life. This was eternity. Irreversible, binding, and utterly final.

We released together. My orgasm triggering his in a cascade that fell like a tidal wave, crashing into the distance.

We lay, panting in the dark of his bedroom. I didn't know what had just happened. It felt like a religious experience. Like I'd found god as I hit the stars on that final note. And I wanted it over and over again.

"Well," Maddox whispered, rolling off of me and onto his back, "how was the date?" He smirked at me. "Do I get a second?"

I tapped my lip contemplatively. "Is it really fair when you know everything about me?"

"I wasn't here to play fair," he said, pulling me against him again. "I was here to win."

"I like this side of you."

"I like every side of you." Then, he flipped me onto my stomach. "Though I am particularly fond of this side."

I laughed but already felt heat building in my core again. I shifted my ass backward toward him. "Perhaps you need a better view."

He smacked my ass with a laugh. "Devious."

"You like it."

He drew my lips to his again. "I do. And I'm taking that second date."

"I was thinking round two."

"You've convinced me," he said with another smirk.

We lost the entire night, and it was glorious.

14

SCAD

SEPTEMBER 29, 2010

"*Happy birthday to Josie! Happy birthday to you!*" the party sang as an elaborate blue-and-gold cake was set before me.

I sat on a chair in my apartment with all of my friends around me. Maddox stood at my side. His smile was effervescent. My roommate, Jamilla, flipped her box braids over her shoulder and gestured forward with her signature long red acrylics.

"Make a wish already, J-Squared," she joked since we were both J first names. We'd become friends sophomore year at a party and never looked back.

I glanced around at the sea of admirers and then to Maddox. I didn't feel like I needed this wish. I had everything I wanted right in front of me. The last two months had been the best of my life. Working all day on my senior thesis film and having sex all night with Maddox. The weekends with our friends on Tybee Island and house parties and River Street and weekend trips to see

Lila at UGA. I'd never known that I could be this happy in a relationship. That they didn't have to be ... work.

We weren't perfect. We still got frustrated with the fact that I would always prefer a party and he'd always prefer a night in. But we'd learned to compromise. I'd shield him from the worst of parties, and he'd take me out when I started getting too jittery, being in one place. He also never minded that I spent time in the gym or went out with my girlfriends or had spa days with Jamilla. Then, he could just *be* in peace. I always had to be going, but he enjoyed the silence. It was a work in progress, and I was enjoying every minute of it.

"Go for it," Maddox said.

So, I closed my eyes and made a wish. A silent plea that things could stay this wonderful forever. Then, I blew out all the candles in one fell swoop. Everyone cheered, and then Jamilla began to cut her masterpiece. She'd been taking cake decorating classes for fun. The things that artists did.

I accepted a piece of the red velvet cake with cream cheese frosting—my favorite—and stepped away from the onlookers to Maddox's side.

"Are you having cake?"

"It was almost too pretty to eat," Maddox said.

"And am I too pretty to eat?" I teased, leaning forward.

His eyes sparkled. "Want to find out?"

"You know I do."

"It is your birthday. It's sort of my duty as your boyfriend."

"I would not disagree."

"This is what I'm thinking," he said, dipping a finger in the cream cheese frosting and bringing it to my lips.

His eyes danced in challenge. And I leaned forward, tasting the frosting on my tongue. I sucked it off his finger. His eyes glazed slightly.

"Now you know exactly what you taste like."

"I was already aware." I took a step closer and dragged one nail over the hardened line of his cock in his pants. "But now, I can see how much I affect you."

"As if you didn't already know."

"Oh, I did," I teased.

His eyes darted around the birthday party. I could tell he already wanted to leave. Whether to fuck me or just to escape the party. "Can we go now?"

I laughed and drew back. "As tempting as that is, no. It's my birthday."

He sighed but didn't argue. "I promise you a more exciting evening."

"I bet."

"And a birthday present."

My eyes widened. "You got me a present?"

He shot me an exasperated look. "It's your birthday."

"Yeah, but ..."

He suddenly looked nervous. "If you don't like it, I can get you something else."

"I haven't even seen it yet, and you're down-talking it. What is it?"

He laughed. "Oh, no. If I have to suffer through the rest of the party, you have to wait for your surprise."

I stuck out my bottom lip. "But I'm the birthday girl."

He drew me into a kiss, dragging that bottom lip into his mouth. "Incentive for us to leave early."

"I guess I'll just have to wait." I pouted half-heartedly.

"I guess you will."

I wrapped my arms around his waist. "I'm glad you're here. I know how much you hate this."

"If you can get me to help you with your film, then you can get me to do anything."

My film. My stomach dropped. That was something I didn't want to think about on my birthday. I loved directing. I'd spent months on my senior thesis film. We were still a month away from it being screened, and there was something wrong. I couldn't put my finger on it, but it wasn't quite right.

Maddox felt me stiffen. "It'll come together, Jos."

"I know," I lied. "It'll be brilliant."

He gave me a disbelieving look and opened his mouth, as if he was going to talk about it more, which was the last thing I wanted tonight, when Jamilla jumped to my side.

"Okay, okay!" Jamilla said. "Break it up, y'all. We have dancing to do."

She winked at Maddox and then hauled me away into the heart of the dance floor. He'd never join me out here unless he was drunk, and since he didn't enjoy being drunk, I would never encourage him to get to that point. I liked him completely sober, slightly judgmental, and always a bit grumpy.

Our friends didn't get it. But I wasn't here for their opinions. I knew it worked, and that was all that mattered.

Still, it was my birthday, and I loved parties. So, I wasn't leaving a second earlier than I had to. The alcohol was flowing, the music was blaring, and I was dancing my ass off with my girls. It wasn't until the wee hours of the morning when the last person finally trickled out of my apartment, and I shut the door. Jamilla kissed my cheek, winked at Maddox, and then disappeared into her room.

I was just past tipsy and threw my arms around his neck. He drew me in close, pressing a kiss into my neck.

"Can I have my present now?" I asked with a giggle.

"Why does it sound like you're not talking about an actual present?"

"Because I'm not."

He shook his head at me. "You might be too drunk for your present."

"Nooo," I groaned. "I'm not that bad. I've had an amazing night." I twirled in place. "I don't ever want this feeling to end."

"All right. Come with me."

We went into my bedroom, and Maddox closed the door behind him. As much as I wanted sex, I was curious as to what someone like Maddox would get me for my birthday. I'd begged Dad not to get me anything. He was struggling so much with work that I knew he couldn't afford it, but he swore he had to get something for his best girl. So, I'd gotten a brand-new camera. As much as I loved and appreciated it, I regretted that he'd spent the money on me. Marley and Lila had sent presents in the mail. Mom had just given me cash, of course.

But Maddox knew me like no one else, and I couldn't help the anticipation.

He had me sit on my bed, and then he went into my closet and removed a large gift. It was roughly a two-by-two-foot square but only a few inches wide and wrapped in brown packing paper. My name was carefully written on a tag at the top. He set it into my grip, but my gaze was still locked on him.

"What is this?"

He gestured self-consciously to the gift. "Open it."

I bit my lip and did as he'd suggested, ripping the paper and revealing the gift hidden within. When the paper fluttered to the ground, I stared down at *myself*. A gasp escaped my lips. It was a portrait drawn in charcoal. My features carefully put on paper. My chin tilted up. My gaze shifted slightly to the left, as if looking out toward the stars. The sharp line of my jaw, strong neck, cut collarbones. My hair as dark as pitch and cascading down one shoulder.

My throat closed as I looked down at the picture that was of me and yet not of me at all. This woman was strong. She was powerful. She was on top of the world. The world was her kingdom, and no one could come near to topple her. But it certainly wasn't me. It was the person I wanted to be.

My eyes locked on the small signature at the bottom of the wood-framed portrait—*M. Nelson*.

"You drew this?" I gasped.

He shot me a worried half-smile. "Yeah. But ... you know ... if you don't like it ..."

"Like it? Maddox, it's incredible. You drew this for *me*?"

"I mean, yeah. I didn't know what to get you. So, I

decided to draw you. The way I see you. The way you talk about your dreams."

Tears glistened in my eyes as I stared up at this incredible man and then down at the portrait. "My dreams?"

"When you talk about what you want to do with your life. You always say that you want to be this big, bold, serious female director. You want to make important films. Films full of the joy and grief of womanhood. That you refuse to be kept out of the conversation just because it has always been a man's world, a man's business. I took those dreams and drew them on the woman that I love."

I gasped softly. "Love?"

His hand came to my jaw, and he pressed a kiss on my lips. "Josie, I love you. I think I've always loved you, but the last couple months have been incredible. You're everything I've ever wanted. And you don't have to say it back," he said quickly, as if he were scaring me off. "But I couldn't hold back how I felt. I want to be there to see you achieve all your big dreams. I want to stand at your side while we take over the world together."

"Shh," I said, pressing a finger to his lips to stop his frantic ramble. "I love you too."

I'd never said those words to anyone before. Not even my parents. We weren't exactly a friendly family like that. Of course, I'd said it to my girlfriends, but that was different. *This* meant something. And it meant as much to me as it did to Maddox.

"You do?"

"I do," I confirmed. "And I love the birthday present."

I hugged it to myself. "You can't take it back or get me anything else. It couldn't be more perfect."

He beamed. "I'm glad you like it."

"Love it," I corrected, putting the portrait on my nightstand. "And you."

Then I kissed him, and we sank back into the bed, where we didn't surface for hours.

15

SCAD

OCTOBER 30, 2010

The audience golf-clapped as the credits rolled.

My face flamed red, and I prayed it wasn't visible beneath the layers of makeup. My hands were clasped behind my back in the sensible black dress I'd purchased for the evening. My feet encased in thousand-dollar shoes that I'd put on my mother's card as a business expense. Not that she'd even noticed. I'd even gotten a blowout for my long black tresses.

And all I felt was humiliation as a pit opened in my stomach and I dropped into it. My film professor said a few words to me as the crowd filed briskly out of the theater. I barely heard what he said. The condescending tone that he'd been using with me all semester hit a fever pitch. I wanted to scream into his face and tell him that his misogynistic good old boys club was bullshit and I didn't want his fucking approval.

It was a lie, of course. I craved approval from everyone around me. Especially the aging dinosaurs that acted as my film profs. Still, none of it changed what had happened here tonight.

"We can discuss this more on Monday, Josephine," the man said.

I shook his hand. I watched him walk away. I swallowed down the bile threatening to come up my esophagus.

"Josie?" Maddox said softly at my side.

I blinked at him. Words wouldn't come. If I opened my mouth, I was going to come undone. I'd start screaming and crying and pulling my hair out, and I wouldn't be able to stop. Four years of film school had led to this moment. Where it should have been my triumph, leading into film festival season. But instead ... I had nothing. Nothing to show for it at all.

"Are you okay?"

I held my hand up. I couldn't even look at him. His short film that I'd voice acted had been shown on Wednesday to critical acclaim. He'd had three job offers on the spot, and the next day, he'd gotten an email ... from Pixar. Maddox was going to be just fine.

I, on the other hand, had no prospects. And even if it wasn't the end of the world, it sure felt as if someone had pulled the rug out from underneath me and I was in free fall.

"Josie, say something. Talk to me. It wasn't that bad."

My eyes snapped to his. A seething glare in them. "Don't," I snapped. He reeled back at the venom in my voice. I hung my head. "Just don't lie."

"I wasn't lying. It wasn't as bad as you're making it out to be. You still have a career in front of you."

"I can't do this."

He opened his mouth to add some more glib, perfunctory platitudes. But I couldn't hear any of it. I couldn't stand here another second. I needed to escape my life going up in flames.

"Josie, come on ..."

"I ... I need a minute."

Then, I grabbed the handle to the back exit and plunged out into the darkened alley behind the theater. I kicked the door behind me and dashed forward to put space between me and everything that had just happened. There were three men in suits at the mouth of the alley, smoking cigarettes. I'd sworn off drugs and smoking since I'd gotten with Maddox. I'd even turned down molly on my birthday. I was not in the mood to be that good girl tonight.

"Hey," I said, strutting toward them. "Can I bum a smoke?"

They broke off their conversation as I approached.

Only one of them was even remotely attractive. A tall guy with long, stringy hair and a snake's smile, who I named Snake in my head. The other two men were older with paunchy bellies, jowls, and lined faces. But even still, I could tell their suits were expensive. The oldest guy was wearing a Rolex, so I named him the same in my head, and the middle guy was No Socks.

"Sure," Snake said, pulling a cigarette out of his pocket and offering it to me.

I put it between my lips and let him light it for me. I winked at him. "Thanks." I leaned back against the brick wall and put one heel back, balancing on one foot. "What a fucking night, eh?"

Rolex eyed me up and down, as if he might offer to pick me up like a prostitute. I was well past the point of caring about anything. I was reeling from the crash and burn of my movie.

"Go on," I said, waving a hand. "Continue your discussion."

No Socks smirked. "Are you here for the festival?"

"Sure am. Would I be dressed like this if I wasn't?" I gestured to my very sensible black dress. The thousand-dollar Jimmy Choos on my feet. Rolex seemed to notice them and gave me a second appraisal.

"Do you work in film?" he asked.

"You could say that."

I blew cigarette smoke into his face. His eyes were clear as he looked back at me, as if he couldn't believe I'd had the audacity. He had money. Big fucking deal.

"We were discussing *Noir*. Did you see it?"

I shot them a Cheshire cat smile. *Noir*. My movie. Lord fucking help me. Of course they were discussing my film.

"Sure," I said, taking another long drag of the smoke. "What a nightmare."

Snake laughed. "Worst thing we've seen here."

"Like, what even was the director thinking?" I added, self-deprecating.

Here was the truth. The absolute truth. Maddox could lie all he wanted, but these men were clearly in the industry. They had no idea who I was. They were being honest.

No Socks shrugged. "At least the CGI was good."

"The only good thing about it," Snake responded.

I nearly huffed. Of course the only good thing about me was Maddox. Classic.

Rolex crossed his arms and eyed me. "You remind me of someone. What did you say your name was?"

"I didn't," I said, stepping away from the wall.

"What does it matter?" Snake asked, clearly ready for this conversation to be over.

I laughed and held my hand out to Rolex. "Josephine Reynolds."

The other two men looked blankly at the name, but Rolex started. Then, his lips curled up. "You're the director for *Noir*."

"At your service."

He guffawed as the other two men looked scandalized. "You have some balls on you," Rolex said.

"Balls are weak actually. Pussy is what can take a pounding."

No Socks snorted, and Snake laughed. But Rolex was still assessing me, looking me over curiously.

"Have you done any acting, Josephine Reynolds?"

I shrugged. "Sure."

"You know who she reminds me of?" Rolex said to his friends.

He took my chin in his hand and held me securely, so he knew that I wouldn't back away. In fact, I lifted my chin in defiance. I'd had a horrible fucking week. I'd sock this man in his fragile nuts if he tried to put a move on me.

No Socks sighed. "Come on. You don't think ..."

"I do," Rolex said.

"Cassie?" Snake guessed.

"Cassie," Rolex agreed.

"Who the hell is Cassie?"

"Henrick," No Socks said to Rolex.

My heart stalled for a full beat. Henrick. My television professor had mentioned briefly that the owner of BFO, the largest family friendly television network in America, would be in attendance. He'd said his name was Henrick Van der Berg. This ... couldn't be ...

Henrick released me with a smirk and withdrew a card from his wallet, passing it to me. "Well, Josephine Reynolds," he said, drawing out my name, "you just got yourself an audition."

"What?" No Socks and I said at the same time.

"She had the worst film at the festival," No Socks growled.

"She's gorgeous, self-assured, and a firecracker. She reminds me of Cassie Herrington, and I want to see her opposite Martin before we make our decision."

My head swam. I couldn't believe this was happening. After the showing I'd had, I'd thought my life was over. Was this real?

The card was heavy with Henrick Van der Berg's name embossed in black, and underneath it was *Berg Family Operations* and a phone number.

"Call the number and speak to my secretary. She'll get you a time to audition."

"Audition for *what*?"

"The lead in my upcoming television show. It's called

Academy. You'll audition in Atlanta, opposite Martin Harper."

I could barely comprehend what was happening. Martin Harper had been my crush since his time on the Disney Channel. I couldn't imagine *meeting* him. Let alone being cast opposite him.

But I saw in Henrick's eyes that the person I already was, was exactly who he wanted this Cassie Herrington to be. The person I'd played my whole life—a cool, confident, flirtatious woman who took no shit. That wasn't even going to be acting. This was ... a break. And I wouldn't squander it.

"All right," I said with a shrug. I stubbed out the cigarette under the toe of my high heel. "Thanks for the smoke."

Henrick smirked at me. "See you soon, Josephine Reynolds."

I could hear No Socks and Snake arguing with him as I walked back down to the stage door. I pulled my phone out of my purse and did some quick research to make sure that this show was actually happening with Martin attached. To my shock, it really was. And all I had to do was call this number to get an audition.

I burst back into the room and nearly ran right into Maddox. "Oh my God, Maddox. You'll never believe what just happened."

His hands came down to my shoulders, and his brows furrowed. "You left twenty minutes ago, near to tears." He looked at my face, flushed with euphoria. "What could have changed your mind that fast?" He frowned. "Did you take drugs?"

"What? No."

He breathed in and wrinkled his nose. "You smell like an ashtray."

"That's not important," I said, brushing past him.

"You smoking again isn't important?"

"I'm not smoking *again*," I said. "I had one cigarette."

"No one has one cigarette, Josie. They're addictive for a reason."

"I had a shit day, Maddox. I had one smoke. Can we move on?"

He ground his teeth together. "Fine. But we're going to talk about this later."

"Looking forward to it," I said with every ounce of sarcasm in my voice.

He bristled at the tone. "Josie—"

"Stop interrupting me," I snapped. "God, let me tell you what happened."

His mouth snapped shut. But his eyes were fiery and pissed. I'd been angry when I left and not let him comfort me, and now, I was back to being my bossy self.

"What happened?" he asked, reaching for calm.

I shoved the card into his hand. "I met Henrick Van der Berg."

"Who?"

"The owner of BFO."

Maddox still looked clueless. Leave it to him to not give a shit about television.

"They have those shows. You know, *Merrymount*, *Honey Town Girls*, *Reality*, *Dean and the Incredible Five*?"

Maddox's frown deepened. "I've heard of *Merrymount*.

Isn't that the show about five girls having sex and doing drugs at a boarding school?"

"Yeah. Well, it's actually about depression and coming out and—"

"It's a dumb teen show," he interjected.

I clenched my jaw. Maddox was shockingly judgmental about most television shows. He'd always said he "never got into it." Whatever that meant. And he certainly didn't like anything that was about normal teenage life. He wanted it to be serious to be good. I really just liked everything. Even if I loved old-timey movies, I still appreciated mainstream success as much as the next person.

"Okay. Well, Henrick offered me an audition for the lead in his next show, called *Academy*." I pulled out my phone and showed him the information. "It's a supernatural school. I'd audition opposite Martin Harper."

"Are you sure this is real?" he asked, disbelieving.

"Yes. I met Henrick himself. I looked him up, too, and it was definitely the guy I'd met. He said that I was perfect for the role."

"Have you considered that he just wanted to fuck you?" Maddox said abrasively.

I glowered at him. "Yes, but he didn't come on to me. He offered me the card and told me to call his secretary." I jumped once in excitement. "It's opposite Martin," I repeated.

Maddox wrinkled his nose again. "You are not using your hall pass."

I held my hands up in frustration. Maddox and I had jokingly offered each other hall passes for our celebrity crushes. If he ever met Cate Kennedy, he could go for it.

And mine had been ... Martin Harper. But I'd never thought I'd actually *meet* him when I said it.

"This isn't about that, Maddox!" I groaned. "You are being nonsensical. I'm not sleeping with Henrick or Martin. I'm auditioning for a major role. This is amazing. It's my big break!"

He looked at me as if I'd sprung a second head. "What part of this is a break for you?"

"I have an audition—"

"But you don't know if you'll get the role."

"Yeah, but—"

"You have no information about any of this."

"So, you think I shouldn't audition?" I snapped right back.

"I wouldn't get your hopes up."

"Wow," I said in shock. "Thanks."

"I'm not saying anything about your acting. I'm saying you were offered this on a whim from a man in an *alley*," he said condescendingly. "You don't know what the fuck this entails." He passed it back to me. "What happened to you wanting to be a serious director?"

"Did you watch my movie?" I demanded.

"Yeah. You're being too hard on yourself."

"People said it was the worst thing at the festival. I'm not being hard on myself. I'm being realistic." I gestured to the card again, my voice rising with my irritation. "This is something tangible. Maybe I won't get the job, but it's better than a half hour ago, when I had nothing."

"This is beneath you."

I reeled back. "What the fuck does that mean?"

"Do you really want to be the star of some teen supernatural-school show?"

"Why not?"

"It sounds ridiculous," he said.

"We're not all as perfect as the incomparable Maddox Nelson," I spat back. "I'm not getting a call from Pixar or getting multiple job offers on the spot. Some of us have to compromise to get what we want."

"This isn't a compromise on what you want. This is driving off the road and crashing into the side of a cliff. You're giving up."

"I'm not giving up."

"Yes, you are. This is what you do. It gets too hard, and you walk away. You said you wanted to do these incredible films, and the first time it doesn't work, you're giving up on it? You're going to take this stupid job and waste all your potential."

"So, that's what you think about me?" I asked as tears came to my eyes.

He thought I ran from hard things. That I couldn't stick it out. He didn't even see it for what it was—the best thing that had ever happened to me. I might not get the job, but I couldn't exactly give up the chance. It was a chance. Just like I'd given to him when he asked me to jump. I hadn't run away because it was hard. I'd been here, fighting for us, for my future. But he didn't see it that way. He didn't see any of it that way.

"Josie, that's not—"

"You think I waste my potential?" I crossed my arms. "God, you are the most judgmental person on the planet. Do you know that? It must be nice to never have to consider having another dream because you're such a goddamn genius that you get everything you've ever wanted in life." I sketched him a mocking bow. "Forgive me for forgetting that no matter what I do, nothing can live up to your impossible standards."

"This has nothing to do with me," he snarled.

"No? Because it sure feels like it has everything to do with you. What if I want this job? What if I want to act? What if I want this *stupid* television show that is *beneath me*?"

"You're overreacting."

I stumbled back at that word. "Wow. No, *this* is overreacting, Maddox." I pushed him lightly in the chest. "We're done."

His jaw dropped open. "What?"

"I can't be with someone who judges every move I make. Who would rather degrade the biggest break of my life than be excited for me."

"Josie," he said, his voice cracking, "please, come on. That's not what I meant at all. Of course I'll support you if this is what you want."

I laughed. "But you didn't care if I wanted it. You were too busy tearing it down."

"I thought we were having a discussion about this."

"For someone who knows me better than anyone else in the world," I said softly, "you don't seem to know me at all."

Maddox's mouth opened and closed in shock at my words. And then I pushed my way back through the stage door. The men in the alley were long gone. And I dropped onto my heels and let the tears fall. The roller coaster of a night finally taking me out until I could barely breathe over the pain of losing everything.

A tear fell on the white cardstock of Henrick's business card, blurring the *G* in his last name. I was going to go to that audition. I was going to meet Martin Harper. And I was going to fucking get that part. I'd prove who I was to the entire world. No one would be able to go anywhere without knowing my name. Only then would I be able to wipe this terrible night from the fires of my life.

PART III

16

SAVANNAH
PRESENT

"Cassie, we'll figure this out together," Martin Harper said to me on the set of the *Academy* movie.

The lights were focused on us. Maddox's incredible visual effects were on the two-hundred-and-seventy-degree screens surrounding us, which displayed the setting, as if we were really standing in Faerie, the world in which *Academy* took place.

My hand went to Martin's chest. I looked up into his impossibly green eyes. "I don't know if I can do this anymore."

Tears welled in my eyes. I could bring them forth with hardly a blink. It was one of the reasons I'd aced the first audition for the show. I'd managed to bring on actual waterworks while opposite Martin. I'd been cast into the lead a week later.

"We can," Martin said.

Then, he dipped his head down, and his lips brushed across mine. They were shockingly familiar. We'd kissed on-screen hundreds of times over the years. Kissed even more times off-screen, tucked away in each other's trailers, lost in each other at our Malibu home, on vacations in between seasons. But *this* kiss was not in the script. It shouldn't have been there at all.

I pushed him away from me, stumbling backward a step. "What the fuck, Marty?"

"Cut!" Jimmy called.

"I was in the moment," Martin said.

"What, like you're a fucking method actor?" I snapped.

Martin stepped back, hurt.

Jimmy strode over in exasperation. This was the third time in the last week that Martin had gone off script because he was 'in the moment.' "Marty, Josie, what is going on?"

"He kissed me again, Jimmy! It's not in the script. Fucking figure this shit out."

"Josie!" Martin cried, just as infuriated with me.

But I stomped off the set before I could listen to his drivel. I passed an irritated Maddox and slumped into my seat. Someone immediately began touching up my makeup. I reached for my water bottle, trying to calm my racing heart.

"Marty, Marty, Marty," Jimmy said, and then I tuned out the oncoming rant.

A throat cleared next to me, and Maddox appeared at my side, computer in hand. His eyes were focused on the screen. I had no idea what he was doing. Some sort of manipulation of the background that would appear on the screen. His tech skills were way beyond me.

"Yes?" I ground out.

We hadn't spoken since last weekend when I'd gone to Gran's house. Since then, we'd seen each other and nodded hello. Perfectly pleasant. But truly, it was hard to pretend that I didn't care about him. And working fourteen-to-sixteen-hour days right now with him always on set was driving me bonkers.

Mars should be in town any minute, which meant we'd be together all weekend. And I still didn't know how to act around him.

"That was some kiss," he said with a smirk on his lips.

"Don't even."

"You called him a method actor." Maddox could barely hold back the laughter. I saw it in his expression. The twinkling of his eyes as he imagined Martin fucking Harper method acting.

I deflated. A laugh left my lips. "God, I can't believe I said that."

"You weren't wrong. He should stick to the script. It's driving Jimmy nuts."

"It's driving *me* nuts."

"I can tell."

I nodded and met his dark gaze. "Any word from Mars?"

"Yeah. She's on her way. Derek wanted to go home first and see his folks. She's dropping him off and then driving out here."

I sighed. "I wanted to meet her in town, but with Martin ad-libbing the entire fucking movie, who knows when we'll get out of here?"

Maddox rested a hand on my shoulder. Sparks flew

between us, and I bit my lip. His face was open and sincere. "You'll get it. You're great at this."

My cheeks heated at the compliment. "I'm surprised that you're even working on this movie. Isn't it beneath you?"

It was a joke, but it came out with more venom than I'd intended. Why had I even said that? It went back to the core of our argument all those years ago. Why was it okay for him to work on this film, but it had been a problem for me in college when I got the audition?

Maddox dropped his hand and sighed. "You know I don't believe that anymore."

"I'm sorry," I said automatically. "I shouldn't have said that. You already told me why you're doing it. We've all had a rough two years."

"I shouldn't have said it was beneath you the first time. The years have proven how wrong I was," he said with a sad twist to his lips. Then, he nodded his head at me and left.

I wanted to follow after him. He'd said hurtful things to me back when I first got the audition. We'd broken up over it. But of course, it hadn't been about the show at all. I followed along with whatever was the path of least resistance, and he forged his own path through the bushes. We'd both ended up right here, but we couldn't have gotten there from more different paths.

"Okay, Josie," Jimmy said, returning to my chair with a conciliatory look on his face. "Can we do it one more time?"

"One more time," I agreed.

It was an hour later when we were finally done, and I could pull my best friend in for a hug.

"You're here!"

Marley hugged me back just as tight. "I missed you."

"Missed you too."

Marley had stood by as I finished up my final lines. Her eyes had been wide with excitement. She was the least excitable person I knew, and even she could be mesmerized by a movie set.

"So, what's the plan?"

Marley was our planner. I knew that though this weekend appeared spontaneous, she would have the entire thing mapped out for us. Which worked fine for me, who was a *go with the flow* sort of person. I just wanted to have as much fun during the holiday weekend as possible and not worry about a thing.

"Well, Derek is at his parents'. He and Amelia and his parents are eating at the Pink House."

"And you aren't? It's the best place in town."

"Eh, I'm letting them have family time. I thought we could chill tonight."

"I'm down. What do you have in mind?"

I was drunk.

That was what she'd had in mind.

I'd followed Marley to Gran's house, where she had promptly raided Maddox's wet bar. Marley only knew how to properly make one drink. So, we'd been drinking Gran's sidecars into the evening until I was giddy and laughing at every single thing she said. We'd video-chatted Lila, who was on her way to Lake Lanier for summer camp for the Falcons. She'd rolled her eyes at us and said she wished that she could be there.

And now, I was slouched on the couch with my feet propped on the coffee table, Walt curled into my side, as if I lived here. Maddox hadn't come home with us. He'd claimed he had hours of edits to do before he could leave, but I thought it was an excuse. I was glad that Marley hadn't said anything about it.

We were halfway into the latest season of *Euphoria* when the door finally cracked open. Of course, there were full-frontal dicks on the television when it happened.

Maddox blinked. "What the fuck are y'all watching?"

Marley burst into laughter and paused the show. Somehow managing to stop it on McSteamy's huge cock.

"Oh my God!" Marley said, pressing play again.

The next time she stopped it was when he was fucking some girl.

"Fuck!" she said and shut the entire TV off.

I burst into laughter, rolling on the floor as tears streamed down my cheeks. Walt jumped from the couch and ran for Maddox, who just shook his head.

"Why are you watching porn on my TV?"

"It wasn't porn," Marley said through her own laughter.

"It was *Euphoria*," I said.

"Ah," he said, closing the door behind him and picking up his dog. "I've heard that's good."

"It is good," I said. "You wouldn't like it though."

He shrugged. "Probably not. How drunk are you? Is there any alcohol left in my house?"

"I can make you a drink," I offered.

He looked down at me, lying on the floor of his house. I'd changed out of my Cassie Herrington getup into short lounge shorts and a tank top. I didn't have to dress up for Mars, but I looked *very* dressed down for Maddox.

He quickly averted his eyes. "I can make it."

"No, no, let me," I said, jumping to my feet and hurrying into the kitchen.

"I'll find something else to watch," Marley said as Maddox followed me.

"Y'all have made yourself at home," he said, dropping his bag on the dining room table. His computer made a clunk on the wood.

He went over to the pantry and scooped out some dog food for Walt, who promptly fell on it like he was starving.

"Well, it's Gran's home," I said. "I've always been more at home here than with my mom."

"What's your mom doing this weekend?"

I shrugged as I poured the liquor for a sidecar. We were running low on the good brandy. "She and her gentleman caller went away on his yacht. Or something."

"Interesting. Do you know who she's dating?"

"I met him briefly earlier in the week."

I had no opinion of the man my mother was currently sleeping with. He wasn't my dad, and that was all I knew. She deserved to be happy after all these years alone, but I couldn't help but feel a knot of betrayal.

"And did you finish her journal?"

I shook my head as I passed him his drink. "I haven't had time with the long hours. I got to the end of her summer. She stopped writing during the first semester at UGA. And it's been hard to keep going."

Maddox took a sip of the drink and coughed. "Shit. I shouldn't have let the drunk girl make my drink."

"What? It's not good?"

"It's strong as hell."

I laughed. "Oh. Well, you need to catch up."

"I'll pass. You and Mars have a good time."

"Okay," I said wistfully as he headed back into the living room with Walt on his heels.

Marley had turned a Pixar movie on. Her head lolled to the side as she watched absentmindedly. Maybe we'd had a little too much to drink.

"Did you work on this one?" Mars asked Maddox.

His eyes skipped to the screen, and he nodded. "Yeah. Before I started my own company." He shook his head at Marley. "Maybe you should drink some water."

"Probably a good idea," she agreed. "I might have to call it an early night. I'm not cut out for this anymore."

Marley stumbled into the kitchen to get water.

"You could stay," I repeated.

"Nah, you have fun."

"Maddox," I said, reaching out for his hand. "Stay."

He let me take it, and sparks flew all over again. I was sober enough to know that I should back off, but I was drunk enough to want to kiss him. Our fingers interlaced for the span of a breath before he released me.

"You're drunk," he said.

"So?"

He sighed. I could feel the conflict in him. He stepped forward, brushing a lock of my hair off of my face. He pressed a kiss to my forehead. "I like having you here."

I listed toward him, wanting nothing more than to let this go further. The alcohol making me even bolder than I already was.

"I like being here with you."

"If only it were that easy," he said with a sharp inhale.

"It could be."

His forehead came to mine. His lips a breath away. I could lift to my tiptoes and claim them for my own.

But then he took a step back. "Good night, Josie."

And I let him go.

"Come on, Walt." He stepped into the downstairs master bedroom with Walt jogging in after him, and the door closed with finality. My heart crumpling at the gesture.

Marley cleared her throat behind me. "Josie?"

My lip quavered for a breath, and I turned to my best friend. "Hey," I said shakily.

"Are you all right?"

I wanted to lie. I wanted to tell her that what had happened didn't matter. I was drunk and acting stupid. Maddox had made it clear that he didn't want anything to happen. I was the one making it worse for him. And I needed to stop.

"No," I whispered.

Marley came and put her arms around me. "What's going on with you two?"

"Nothing."

"You look too hurt for nothing."

"He just ... he doesn't want anything from me anymore."

Marley laughed softly as she stroked my hair. "No, Josie, that isn't true. He wants it more than anything. You just have a rough history. And you need to figure out how to trust each other again."

"He said we're too different."

"Maybe you are," she whispered. "But Derek and I are complete opposites, and we made it work. So, if you want to make it work, then you're going to have to figure it out."

My resolve hardened. The spark between us was still there. He felt it. I felt it. I couldn't live with myself without seeing if we could do this one more time. No matter what our history said, I would prove to him that I was second to none.

17

SAVANNAH
PRESENT

Derek flopped down onto the towel next to Marley. "Are you going to sit here all day?"

She put her hand in her husband's face. "Yes. Now, stop bothering me while I read."

I snorted as I lathered another layer of tanning oil on my legs. Technically, I wasn't supposed to change my appearance between one week and the next for the film, but that was what makeup was for.

"You've already read that book before," he said, reaching for it. "Isn't that the sexy Fae male alphaholes?"

"Derek Ballentine, so help me God." She jerked the book away from him.

He only gave her an insufferable smirk and dropped his sweaty Carolina-blue UNC hat onto her head. She was already entirely hidden under an umbrella, so she wouldn't lobster. The hat was merely a taunt, considering she had gone to Duke.

"Ew! Gross, Derek." She flung the hat off into the sand.

"You love me."

"Yes, but none of us know why," I muttered.

Marley chuckled. "For real."

"Because I'm irresistible," he said, lounging back against her legs. "Obviously."

"Obviously," Marley said with an eye roll.

Maddox snorted from his seat opposite us. He'd gone into work for a few hours and then met us at the beach in the afternoon when Ash and Amelia showed up. He'd been sketching in his notebook and drinking the beer that Ash had brought in a cooler.

Up until Derek had plopped down, Amelia had been tanning with me, and Ash had been throwing a football with Derek. But Amelia wanted to go in the water despite what was surely too cold temperatures for me, but Ash had obliged. She was currently squealing as the water lapped at her thighs. Ash looked like a sun-kissed god as he strode into the water, unperturbed.

"Why didn't you get in the water?" Marley asked Derek. "Then, you wouldn't be bothering me."

"I prefer to be *on* the water, not *in* the water, Minivan," he said, the nickname dripping with affection. "That's why we're going sunset sailing tonight."

"I prefer to be indoors," Maddox said under his breath.

I couldn't help it; I laughed. "Oh, you poor baby introvert."

Another scream ripped from the water, and we all turned to watch Ash tackle Amelia into the oncoming wave. They came up, sputtering. Amelia slapped him across the chest. Whatever she said to him was lost to the wind.

The three of us slowly turned to look at Derek. We'd been waiting all morning to see if he'd realize what was happening with them. They'd been friendly all day. But I knew Ash Talmadge, and I knew what he looked like when he was into someone. I'd watched him with Lila my entire life. And though I doubted he'd ever look at anyone like he looked at Lila, I could tell that he was falling for Amelia.

And we were waiting for Derek to see it too.

"What?" he asked. "Why are you all looking at me like that?"

Maddox finally sighed. "Do you not see what is right before your eyes?"

"My sister and best friend are in the water."

Marley covered her face with her book and giggled.

"He's into her," I filled him in.

Derek sighed. "Yeah, I gathered."

"And you're okay with it?" Marley gasped.

"No," he said, heat in his voice. "But also ... yes. It depends."

"On what?" I asked.

"Lila."

We all sighed at once. Didn't it always come back to the lovely Delilah Greer?

"Man, I thought you were going to get in a fight today," I said with a laugh.

He shook his head. "Nah. Ash knows where I stand regarding Mia. I wouldn't fucking care if they dated. But ..."

"But Lila," Marley finished.

"Yeah."

Ash Talmadge had loved one person, and he'd spent his life chasing her. Lila being happy with someone else hadn't stopped him from falling back into her orbit over and over again. Two years wasn't long enough to know whether or not it would last. I wouldn't wish Ash Talmadge on anyone until he was over her. If he could ever get over her ...

"Oh my God," Amelia gushed when she reached our setup in the sand. She grabbed her towel and wrapped it around her body as her teeth chattered. "It is too cold for that."

"You're the idiot who wanted to go in there," Derek pointed out.

Amelia rolled her eyes. "Thanks, ass."

"Ash didn't seem to care," I pointed out.

He was striding back toward us, but he didn't even look cold.

"He doesn't count," Amelia said.

But her eyes landed on him, and she was drinking him up. Because the secret I knew was that Amelia Ballentine had been into Ash for all those years he was into someone else. She might be able to hold him off for a little while, but she didn't want to hold him off forever.

"So, how's the movie going, *Josephine*?" Ash asked when he dropped into a seat next to Amelia.

I eyed him skeptically. "You really want to know?"

"I asked," he said simply.

We'd had our differences, but he seemed sincere. So, I

started talking about the movie. I even got Maddox in on the conversation.

It shifted the whole afternoon until we were all sharing about our latest endeavors. Until Derek said it was time to pack up and get to the sailboat. I could tell he was anxious.

"Count me out," I said with a smile. "The smallest boat I want on is a yacht."

"Oh, come on," Marley said. "It's not that bad."

"Seasickness," I said. "I'm out. You have fun."

"Me too," Maddox said. "I should probably get home to Walt anyway. I could drive you to your place."

I beamed. "I'd like that."

Marley pouted. "But I'll see you tomorrow?"

"Definitely," I said, giving her a big hug.

We packed everything up and headed across the bridge that led over the dunes and to Maddox's Jeep. He dropped the beach chairs and towels into the back and his bag in the backseat before we got inside.

"Thanks for driving," I said.

"It's not a problem."

"What were you sketching?"

He dug into the bag in the back and passed me the sketchbook. "Mostly work."

I flipped through it. No longer was it full of pictures he'd doodled of me from college, and his art skills had been honed to a razor's edge. He was *good*. Before, he'd always say that he dabbled. Charcoal was no longer his medium of choice, and the pencil sketches he'd been working on came to life before my eyes.

It was the set of *Academy*. The forests of Faerie, faerie

pools, and the great, towering academy that was the fore-front of the show. I flipped to the next page when I found a picture that was clearly of me in the forest with tears in my eyes.

"This is ... amazing, Maddox."

"It helps me visualize what I want on the computer before I have to do the visual effects."

"I wish I could do something like this."

Maddox shot me an incredulous look. "Have you seen yourself act? You're a natural."

"Yeah, but it's not ... art. It's easy."

"And *that* is easy for me," he said, gesturing to the notebook. "What you do is art too. I could *never* act. Frankly, I'd never want to be in front of a camera at all if I could help it."

"That's true," I said with a laugh. "So, what's next for you after you finish *Academy*?"

"Ugh. I don't know," he said, his grip on the steering wheel tightening. "There's a new superhero movie that the studio wants me to work on. But it's out in LA, and LA drains me. I prefer the projects that come to Savannah. Georgia has such good breaks for the film studios. It makes more sense to be out here anyway."

"Says the introvert," I joked.

"Yeah. And what about you? What's next for Josephine Reynolds?"

I shrugged, looking down at my hands. I hadn't told anyone about this yet. But if I couldn't be vulnerable with Maddox, then how could I ever get past the wall we were up against? "Well, I have an audition next weekend in

Atlanta. It'll be a quick trip, but my manager set it up before I got the call about *Academy*."

"Same kind of thing?"

My heart brushed aside the cobwebs and hoped again. "No, it's, uh ... it's an experimental indie film with a female director about a woman who takes on her sister's kids after an overdose and the weight of dealing with the teenage youth's own opioid addiction."

Maddox straightened at those words. His gaze swept to me with awe in them. "That sounds ... amazing."

"I thought so too. And it's a mostly female cast, female director, producers, the works. It's going to be shot on film and not digitally. I even got word that it might be shot in black and white."

I went giddy at the thought. I'd been auditioning for a lot of stuff since *Academy* had finished, but this was the first one that I really wanted. It was the direction I'd wanted to go since I was young. And the part felt important.

"That sounds exactly like what you always wanted to be doing. Except you wanted to be that director."

"I know. One step at a time."

"One step at a time."

Maddox pulled the truck in front of my mom's house. It was huge and empty. And truly the last place I wanted to go inside.

We'd had a nice day at the beach. It had been like the good old days. Almost like anything was possible. Like I could invite Maddox inside for a drink and it would bloom into more. Like our friendship could turn into what it once had been.

I wanted to give him that invite. I wanted to be bold, brave Josie. But he'd rejected me. He'd told me to my face that it wasn't going anywhere. It was hard to keep pushing when he seemed to have finally moved on.

I chickened out, ready to say good night.

"Josie," he said, drawing my attention back to him.

Then, he was there. His fingers pushed up into my hair, tugging me the short distance across the Jeep. His mouth settled on mine, and everything quieted. Those lips were oh-so familiar. Warm and wet and responsive. His tongue slipped across the seam of my lips, and I opened to him with ease.

Our tongues moved together. A flick to test the waters and then a dance that we'd spent long nights perfecting. I reached for him, my hand circling his bicep and trying to drag him closer.

I had no idea how this had happened. I'd almost given up. But here he was, shattering all my expectations. Kissing Maddox was effortless, like breathing.

I could have lived in that moment forever, but slowly, he withdrew. He placed one more kiss on my now-swollen lips. And I pushed forward, stealing more.

"Mmm. I could have another one of those."

He laughed and released me. "Same."

"Well, you didn't have to stop."

"I should get home."

"Or you could come in," I whispered hesitantly. He brought my fingers to his lips and kissed them. "Why did you change your mind?"

"I didn't," he said automatically.

"You said we were too different."

"But when I'm with you, it feels like we're the same."

My heart melted at those words. "Me too."

"I couldn't decide if I was doing the right thing by staying away from you after all our baggage. Or if I was being a fool for letting you go when you're right here."

"What did you decide?"

He kissed me again, quick and decisive. "Both."

"It can't be both."

"I know. But you're here, and I can't stay away from you. I've never been able to stay away from you. So, I kissed you."

"What does that mean going forward?"

"It means I want to kiss you again."

"More than kiss me?" I teased.

He arched an eyebrow. "Obviously."

"Then, come to Atlanta with me next weekend."

"For your audition?"

I nodded. "I'm going to see my dad and hang out with Lila and Cole. Maybe we need some space from all of ... this." I gestured to Savannah, which held so many memories, so much history between us. I couldn't look around and not see Maddox in every city block.

His eyes dipped to my mouth again. He conceded with a nod. "All right. We'll see how this goes."

I felt like we were repeating history with that phrase, but I swore it wouldn't all end the same way this time.

"Sure you can keep your hands to yourself until then?"

He smirked, and it looked hot as fuck on him. "Well, maybe one more kiss then."

And our lips crashed back together.

18

HARVARD

NOVEMBER 22, 2012

I t was two years before Maddox and I were in close proximity again.

After our ill-fated breakup, we had finished out our senior year entirely separate. I'd gotten the job for *Academy*, which filmed primarily in south Atlanta. And he'd taken the Pixar job and moved to LA.

As much as I'd hated his comments, I wouldn't pass up the opportunity to see Marley when she invited me to her Friendsgiving at Harvard. Girl was a genius, and I loved seeing her in her element. But when she'd told me that Maddox was coming, I'd almost canceled.

Two years. It had been two *years* since I'd seen him. It felt unfathomable.

Still, a part of me *wanted* to see Maddox. I'd done what he'd said wasn't going to happen. I was the star of a hit TV show. I'd filmed two seasons of *Academy* with Martin Harper, and I was no longer doe-eyed around him. He was just my costar ... and boyfriend, if you believed the tabloids.

And I had no idea how today was going to go.

I straightened my spine, put on my best smile, and knocked on my best friend's door. A second later, I heard running steps, and then Marley was in front of me.

I launched myself at her. "Mars!"

She laughed. "Hey, Josie. I missed you."

"I missed you too!" I withdrew and looked her up and down. "So, tell me everything. Boys?"

"Nope. No boys. Mostly work."

I rolled my eyes at her. "Ugh, lame. Come to LA and have fun with me sometime." I knocked my hip into hers as I rolled my suitcase into her little apartment. "All work and no play makes Marley a dull girl."

"I think you and Lila have enough boy troubles for the lot of us."

I brushed my hair off my shoulder. "I am not having troubles. I'm in a perfectly great relationship right now."

"With your costar," she murmured under her breath.

So the tabloids said. Well, that was what I wanted to say, but I couldn't exactly deny it. Martin and I had great chemistry on- *and* off-screen. We'd been caught canoodling at a Beverly Hills hotel, and suddenly, ratings for *Academy* went up. Overnight, the studio and our publicists crafted some perfect off-screen role for us. And it was easy at first since we'd been hooking up anyway. But making it a business arrangement had killed the romance for me. And though I liked him ... I could never quite decide whether or not I could love him.

But I wasn't prepared to lay that out for anyone. Let alone Marley, who was frankly as judgmental as her brother and would think the whole thing was absurd.

"Hey!" I said. "There's nothing wrong with that. It's why our chemistry is great."

"If you say so." Marley arched an eyebrow. She didn't buy it for a second, and how could I blame her? "And where is the inimitable Martin Harper?"

I waved my hand. The last thing I wanted was for Marty to be here. "Busy. We have plans for Christmas."

I had off from work between now until then. He was filming some short film in the meantime for a friend, but we'd planned to be photographed together right before the holiday. My assistant had sent over outfit suggestions yesterday. Sometimes, this life was exhausting.

"Look who arrived."

I turned at the sound of Maddox's voice. He was standing in the entrance to a bedroom in nothing but a pair of athletic shorts. I couldn't look away. His shoulders had broadened. He'd clearly been working out. His hair was dripping wet, his unmistakable curls utterly tempting me to run my fingers through them. Even as he pulled a T-shirt overtop his chest, I couldn't stop my eyes from roaming over him.

"Hey, Maddox," I said with a soft smile.

But Maddox did not look pleased to see me. Marley had to have warned him. She knew all about our problems in college. Yet he crossed his arms over his chest and stared me down.

There was anger in his eyes and venom in his voice when he said, "The superstar has graced us with her presence."

I didn't wince at his words. I was too good of an actor

to show that he'd hurt me. But Marley was looking between us like she'd never seen us before.

"Anyway!" Marley said loudly, breaking the tension. "I'm going to check on the turkey. People should be here shortly. Josie, you can dump your stuff in my room. We'll figure out the sleeping situation later."

"Sure," I said. I grabbed my suitcase in one white-knuckled hand and brushed past Maddox without a word.

I took deep breaths in Marley's bedroom. It was one day with him. I could get it together. I was here for Marley, and that was all that mattered.

I changed out of my airport clothes and into a cute dress. I checked my phone one more time and smiled at the text from my dad. It was a picture of him in an apron that read *Kiss the Cook* with the other employees from the art studio around him.

After I'd started bringing in real money from *Academy*, I'd funneled it to my dad. He'd tried to give it back when I first started making deposits to his account, but I'd hated those years in college when he couldn't support himself. I had more than enough money to go around. I wouldn't let him continue to suffer like that when I had the means to make it stop. He'd reopened the art studio. And though it wasn't doing *well*, it was doing better than it had when he had to close it while I was in college.

He looked happy now. So much happier than he'd been in years.

I shot off a *Happy Thanksgiving* text and then hurried into the kitchen.

Right before dinner was ready, there was a knock on the door, and Marley went pale.

"I'll get it."

I shot her a look and kept an eye on the door. And to my shock, in walked Derek Ballentine. Well, well, well ... maybe Marley wasn't so anti-boy either. In fact, my bestie looked *smitten* with this Holy Cross boy. What in the world?

When we got a break in the conversation, I followed Marley back into the kitchen. "So ..." I said, leaning against the counter as Mars carved the turkey up.

"Yeah?"

I shot her a look. "That's Derek Ballentine."

"I know who it is."

"What secrets have you been keeping from me?"

"None," she said, immediately going on the defensive.

I laughed. Oh, this was going to be good. "He's so into you, Mars. Are y'all sleeping together?"

"No!"

But she'd said it a little too quickly. So, I crossed my arms and waited for her to dish.

"Well, not anymore."

"I knew it!" I cried. Oh my God, my little Marley, all grown up.

Then, she gushed about how they'd hooked up in college and how he wanted them to get back together, but she was sure they were *just friends*. It was hard to keep from rolling my eyes at them. They were *not* just friends. The way he looked at her was as if she was a dream come true. It was frankly disconcerting. I'd only ever had one boy look at me like that, and he was currently talking up Derek.

"Just ... don't tell Lila," Marley begged.

I shook my head. Oh, she was in a heap of trouble. And I hated keeping secrets from Lila. That never turned out well.

"Fine, but you owe me one."

She bit her lip, like she'd like anything else but to owe me a favor, but she must have really meant it because she nodded and said, "Fine."

Thanksgiving was delicious, and Marley's Harvard friends were so friendly. Her roommate happened to be a huge *Academy* fan, and I made sure to only sneak looks at Maddox once to see his reaction to her roommate gushing about my job. But he was purposely looking down and saying nothing.

By the time dinner was over, my entire body was on edge. This should have been my triumphant moment, and instead, I felt ... empty.

I was glad when everyone else left. Marley's roommate gave me her bedroom for the night. Maddox was taking the couch.

"I'll just be a minute," Marley said as she stepped outside with Derek.

When the door closed, Maddox and I were officially alone together. The silence was interminable. I wanted to shake something loose in him. Have him *look* at me or fucking say something. Fuck.

"She's into a Holy Cross boy. Who would have guessed?"

Maddox shrugged. "She liked him in high school."

My eyes widened. "Wait ... what? She said college."

"I drove her to his house once."

My gasp made him finally look up at me. "How did I never know this?"

"You know Mars."

I did. But now that his dark eyes were on me, I wasn't thinking about my bestie at all.

"It's good to see you, Maddox."

He clenched his jaw. "I'm sure."

"Maddox ..."

"You got everything you ever wanted, Josie. I don't really want to have this conversation."

I nodded, swallowing back my own anger rising in me. "Fine."

Marley rescued us by stepping back inside. She had a drowsy, lovesick look on her face. "That was fun."

"Totally."

Putting on a fake smile, I turned back to Mars and pretended Maddox didn't matter at all. I felt him with us the entire time we enjoyed the night. Marley must have felt the tension. It was thick and toxic in the room, but she let us be. At least she was good for that.

Marley promised to walk me around Harvard tomorrow and then went into her room and closed the door. I went into her roommate's room and lay in her bed, staring up at the popcorn ceiling. Maddox was a room away, and I could still feel the anger bristling between us. As potent as ever.

"Fuck."

I didn't want things to be like this. I didn't want any of this.

19

HARVARD

NOVEMBER 23, 2012

Kicking my feet over the side of the bed, I pulled a cardigan over my tank top and stepped hesitantly out of the bedroom. Maddox was asleep on the couch. Damn, how had he gone to sleep so easily? Why wasn't he fuming as much as me?

I poured myself a glass of water. As I went to return to the room, I heard his voice say softly in the dark, "Josie?"

I jumped, and water sloshed onto the rug. "Shit."

"What are you doing?"

"Getting water."

He sat up on the couch, shifting enough to reveal that he was in nothing but boxers and a loose T-shirt. My throat bobbed. God, he was handsome in a completely unruffled way. The opposite of every guy I'd met since moving to LA.

"Want something stronger?"

I bit my lip, wondering what the catch was, but still, I nodded. He got to his feet and went into the kitchen, appearing a minute later with two glasses of amber liquid.

"Thanks," I said, taking a sip from the drink. I winced. "Whoa, what is this?"

"Whiskey and Coke. Marley only has cheap whiskey and brandy." He shrugged. "Best I could do."

I remained standing as he plopped back down on the couch. I was shivering where I stood in shorts. The California girl who had forgotten how cold Massachusetts winters were.

"You don't have to stand there and freeze. I won't bite."

"That's debatable," I said. "You sure had some biting words to say about my career."

He sighed and tipped back the drink. "Yeah. I guess I'm bitter."

"For being wrong?" I shot back.

"For losing you."

The malice left my voice at that admission. I walked the few steps to the couch and took a seat next to him, stealing the blanket and wrapping it around my bare legs.

"I know what you mean," I finally said.

His eyes were still locked on me, almost as if he couldn't believe we were sitting here. "Is that so? Off dating the man of your dreams and you want me to believe that you've thought of me?"

"I thought you weren't going to bite."

"Yeah. I guess I sort of hate Martin Harper."

"That's fair," I admitted.

He'd been our joke. A hall pass if I ever met him. And while he wasn't the reason Maddox and I had ended, it had to be salt in the wound that I was with him now.

"Marley mentioned you were seeing someone," I said softly.

He shook his head. "Nah. We've gone on a few dates, but I don't know. Nothing special."

"I see."

"And Martin?" Maddox forced out.

"He's great. We're great," I said, but even I could hear the fake sound of my voice. The charade was so hard to keep up with someone who knew every crack in my heart.

Maddox looked confused. "What's going on, Josie?"

My shoulders slumped forward. "I was dating Martin. Or whatever." I bit my lip. "You know, we were sneaking around. But then the pictures were out in the tabloids, and suddenly, it became ... work."

"Work?" he asked in confusion.

"It was more a publicity stunt than anything."

Maddox's eyes widened. "You're not really together?"

"We were. But when it became work, I don't know ... it felt so Hollywood. Like another thing that I had to put on a smile for. We started planning our appearances, and Martin is a nice guy, but he's not ..." I shrugged, not even sure how to finish that sentence.

"You shouldn't have to act in your personal life, Josie."

I shouldn't have to, but I had been my entire life. It was only in Savannah that I felt like I could really be myself. Hollywood didn't want small-town Josie. They wanted Josephine Reynolds.

"Easy for you to say," I said with a laugh as I set my

empty whiskey glass down. "Ratings for *Academy* were through the roof when they caught us. More people watch every time we're photographed together. Being with Martin, whether real or not, helps my career."

Maddox downed the rest of his drink and put it next to mine. "The show had record-breaking numbers before this. Don't sacrifice your happiness for a TV show."

As much as I wanted to listen to him, it was that simple.

"Hey," he said, taking my jaw in his hand and turning me to face him.

Blood pounded in my ears at that one touch. My body waking up after a long sleep. Only his hand on me could make me feel this immediately desperate for more.

"Listen to me. You don't have to be with anyone to help your career. That is Hollywood getting to you. What would you say to Marley or Lila if something like this happened to them? You'd go to bat for them. I know you would."

"True, but ..."

"You're the star," he said softly, mesmerizingly. "Be with whoever you want, Jos."

And that nickname on his tongue undid me. I crushed our lips together. He made a small noise of surprise and pulled back slightly.

"Are you sure?" he asked, as if he were the one to force himself on me and not me jumping him.

"Please," I whispered.

"Fuck."

Then, his hands were in my hair, dragging our lips back together. He tasted like whiskey and smelled like home. Kissing him felt more right than anything else I'd ever done in my life. I'd forgotten that anything could feel like this. That Maddox could make everything disappear.

He pushed me down into the couch. His body covered mine. The solid weight of him as I wrapped my legs around his waist made me shiver with need. I could tell through the thin material of his boxers how much he'd missed me. Our limbs tangled, our tongues volleying for control, our hips meeting like they had so many times in the past.

"Oh God," I gasped as he pushed his pelvis against me.

His hand came to my mouth. "Shh," he breathed.

And somehow, that one command made me even wetter. I'd forgotten where we were. That his sister was one door over while we christened her couch.

"Are you going to be quiet?" he asked with a gleam in his eyes.

I nodded my head, and he slowly removed his hand, dragging it down my body.

"I have doubts about your ability to be silent," he said with a smirk. "We'll see how good you can be."

Before I could say anything at all, he slid down my front, gripping my tiny shorts and ripping them down my legs. His mouth fell on my pussy. And I had to clap a hand over my own mouth to muffle my moans.

His tongue laved over my clit as he swirled two fingers through the wetness at my core. And fuck, he remembered exactly how I liked it. He sped up the tempo of his tongue as my breathing turned labored. He slowly eased two fingers the rest of the way inside of me. I arched backward on the couch. A flush started at my neck and flooded down the rest of my body.

He sucked my clit into his mouth as he started a tempo, in and out. I'd forgotten how attentive he was to every hitch in my breath and shift of my hips and curl of my toes. He sped up when my breathing began to even, forcing me to teeter on the edge of an orgasm.

"Oh," I gasped as he roughly forced my legs wider.

"Shh," he said, looking up at me from between my legs.

My body heated up just at the sex-crazed look in his eyes. Then, he dipped his head back down to his mission and didn't stop until my muscles contracted and I came on his fingers and into his mouth.

I turned my head into the pillow to try to keep my whimpers to myself. I had no idea how successful I was.

Then, Maddox was stepping out of his boxers and sliding on a condom. "That was good," he said, and I shivered.

"It was amazing."

He sank back down onto the couch and pulled me up. "Come get a taste."

I stood on shaky legs as I arranged myself on his lap, poised over his cock. His lips found me, and I tasted my own come. We both groaned as he sank me inch after inch onto him. When I was finally seated on him, I released a sharp breath.

"There you are," I sighed. I rested my hands back on his knees and tipped my head back. "That's the spot."

His hands ran up my sides, under my shirt, and over

my breasts. My cardigan was loose, falling off my shoulders. My long black hair fell like a curtain behind me.

"You're a vision," he murmured as he shifted a little further up into me, causing me to gasp softly.

I rolled my hips, undulating on him as temptingly as possible. It was his turn to dig his hands into my hips.

"Tease," he said.

I looked into his eyes with a smile. "Is it a tease if your cock is currently inside of me?"

"Absolutely."

"Would you have it any other way?"

"This way."

And then he used the grip on my hips to lift me off of him and slam me back down. It was *not* a quiet sound, but at this point, I was already back on the edge. I hoped Mars was fast asleep and couldn't hear what we were doing, because I was enjoying myself too damn much to stop now.

The years had separated us. Pride and ego and far too much judgment. But we were here, in this place, together again. And I couldn't think of anywhere else I'd ever want to be again.

"Fuck, Josie," he said, tugging me close against him. Our chests pressed tight. His eyes looking up into mine with adoration on his face.

I met each thrust with a forceful downward motion. Our slaps were definitely louder than they should have been. My orgasm rushed up to my body without warning.

"Oh God," I whispered.

"Yes. Now," he commanded as we came together.

I gasped into Maddox's shoulder. My body trembled,

and I shuddered on top of him. His grip tightened around me, holding me close as we both came down.

I found his lips and pressed a delirious kiss on them. "Wow," I whispered.

"Yeah." He kissed me again.

I slowly eased off of him. We both used the bathroom, and when I returned, he opened his arms wide, and I slid into place in front of him.

"I missed you," he said against my ear.

"I think that was obvious."

"You missed me too."

"I did," I said.

"What are you going to do when you get home?" he asked as if it physically pained him to do so.

I turned to face him and let my hands run through his curls like I'd wanted to do when I first walked in. "I'll talk to Martin. You're right. It's my life, right?"

"It is."

"And you?" I asked, biting my lip.

"I'll be in LA in the new year for a movie."

"Yeah?" I asked, hope rising in my chest. "I'll be in Georgia, filming again, in April. We could ... we could see how it works."

He pressed a kiss to my forehead. "You don't know how much I want that."

I released all the tension in my body. I'd come here, expecting Maddox to hate me. For me to hate *him* for what had happened in the past. And in the end, I'd realized what I'd always known ... that he was the one for me.

20

MALIBU

DECEMBER 22, 2012

I had no idea how I was supposed to break up with Martin.

I'd tried to convince him to delay our big publicity shoot at Moonshadows in Malibu, where I was currently pacing the restroom. But he wouldn't hear of it. He was back in town and wanted to celebrate with his girl. His words.

There had been no way to decline without breaking up with him over the phone. And he deserved better than that. I hadn't seen him since before I'd left for Thanksgiving. He'd been filming in Croatia. The time difference between that and the West Coast was terrible. It had been hard to find time to talk, let alone break up with him.

I'd promised Maddox that this was our last event. That I would get through dinner and then break it off once we left.

Not that Maddox was particularly pleased that I was still attached. We'd been talking most nights. I'd been tempted to fly out to Savannah to see him, but I needed to handle Martin first. God forbid the press found out that I was seeing someone else. It would be a nightmare.

So, I'd gone along with Martin's plan. My stylist had sent over a stunning champagne dress that highlighted my tan skin and fit my body like a glove. I was in thousand-dollar shoes. My hair and makeup had been professionally done. Photographers would be on standby to snap a picture of our perfect moment. I had to make it through one little dinner, and then this would all be over.

With a breath, I pushed through the restaurant and out to the ocean-view dining. Heat lamps were on for the chilly December evening. Martin stood as I approached the cabana-style bed he'd reserved for us. Or more likely, his assistant had reserved for us. A perfect place to be seen.

"Darling," Martin said, drawing me in close and pressing a hungry kiss on my lips.

"How was your trip?"

Martin grinned, taking me in. "First, look at you. Jesus, Josephine, did you get more gorgeous since I left?"

"Hair and makeup," I assured him with a laugh.

He moved his finger in a circle, and I turned for him, giving him a private show. We settled onto the cushions, and he snapped his fingers at a waiter.

"French 75, right?" he asked, remembering my favorite drink.

I'd fallen in love with the drink the night we'd gone skydiving and he'd insisted we try this speakeasy in the middle of nowhere. He ordered me one everywhere we went from then on. It was something about the gin and champagne, mixed with the sweet lemony flavor, that brought me right back to why I'd fallen for Martin in the first place ... and not just the boy I'd swooned over on the television in high school.

As soon as my drink arrived, Martin launched into the most fascinating tale of the new film he'd spent the last two months working on.

And that was the thing about Martin—he was fascinating. Everything he did was a fun, new adventure. He wanted me to be part of every one of those journeys too. It was how we'd started. He'd gotten me to go skydiving with him. Then, we'd surfed on a private Malibu beach. Then, he'd flown me to Hawaii on a whim to snorkel and see a waterfall. It was a miracle that our first appearance together had been here in LA. We'd lived a crazy, private life before then. That was the Martin that I'd seen myself falling in love with. Not the one who acquiesced to see me when his publicist could fit me into his busy schedule.

By the time the first course came, I'd forgotten my earlier apprehension. Martin talked enough for the both of us. I didn't even have to pretend to enjoy his company because I did. He was charming, personable, the heart of any party. In fact, he was my perfect complement.

Anyone would think I was insane for giving him up for the guy who'd broken my heart in college. And yet I always had this suspicion that Martin couldn't love anyone more than he loved himself.

"My sweet," he said, tipping my chin with his knuckles.

"What was that?"

"You went somewhere far away."

I laughed to cover my discomfort. "Sorry. It's hard to believe you're home. It's been so long."

"I've been monopolizing the conversation. Tell me what you've been doing. You visited your little friend from home while I was gone, yes?"

I bristled at him describing Marley as my little friend from home but didn't let that show. "Yes, Marley. We grew up together. She had Thanksgiving at her apartment in Cambridge with her brother and friends."

"That's adorable," he said. "Thank God we're not apartment living anymore, eh?"

I laughed softly. "Absolutely. I don't miss that at all."

Which was true. But I hated that he always put down people who made less than us. Marley was going to change the world. Who cared where she lived?

"Well, I'd like to meet all of these childhood friends of yours."

"You would?" I asked skeptically.

That didn't sound like Martin. He was all about the next big and better, not about the past. It was why he had no idea that the brother that I'd mentioned was Maddox or any of our history. It didn't concern him, so it didn't matter.

"Of course. Maybe after the holidays, we can go visit, and I can meet these mysterious friends. Marley, and the other one is ... Delilah?"

I blinked in surprise. "Uh, yes. Delilah. We call her Lila."

He snapped his fingers. "I knew it. You'd like that, wouldn't you?"

"I would," I said uncertainly.

But I was also confused. As much as I liked Martin, I'd always felt like our lives were separate. There was a line in the sand that was before and after *Academy*. And the before had never mattered to him.

"Good. Good," he said. "I want everything with you, Josephine Reynolds."

I narrowed my eyes. He was repeating those words to himself, like he did on set when he was remembering memorized lines. Was this whole thing just an act for him? What the hell?

But before I could ask what was going on, Martin slid off of the cushion and dropped to one knee before me.

My mouth popped open in shock. "Martin!"

He withdrew a red box with a Cartier diamond inside. My hand flew to my mouth. Oh my fucking God, he was proposing. This couldn't be real. We had never discussed the future. I couldn't believe he was doing this. Had this even been his idea?

"Josephine, would you make me the happiest man in the entire universe and marry me?"

I wanted to make a scene. I wanted to storm off, caught in this riptide of confusion. Truly, I had no idea how any of this was happening. What had made Martin decide to take this step? We'd been seeing each other for almost a year, but I'd never had the inclination that he wanted to settle down. That we were serious enough for this.

But I could do none of what I wanted. There were cameras everywhere. He'd picked this very public display to get the best angle on his proposal. It was why he wouldn't listen to me asking to meet before we had this big, fancy dinner. He'd planned this.

"Josie," he said softly when I stared down at him in shock.

And in those eyes, there was real emotion. Martin hadn't been talking relentlessly tonight because he wanted to hear himself speak. He'd been nervous. He'd been preparing himself, and he wanted this. It might look like a stunt, but I could see the sincerity in his eyes.

"I've never met anyone else like you. I'll never know anyone who is so much like me. I love you. Marry me."

Tears came to my eyes. As they always did when I called them forth. I'd gotten the job for *Academy* with these tears, and, Jesus, they should give me an Academy Award for the ones that sprang up right now.

"Yes," I gasped because there was nothing else I could say.

I threw my arms around him, and then his mouth was on mine, pressing a firm, hopeful kiss on my lips. He withdrew long enough to slide the enormous haloed ring on my finger. It glittered and shimmered as brightly as the sunset over the California coast.

I smiled for the cameras as if this were the best moment of my life. All the while, my stomach twisted in fear. All I knew was that I needed to talk to Maddox before this got back to him.

It was hours later before I was alone again in the safety of the bedroom at the Beverly Wilshire. Martin had booked us the penthouse to celebrate our engagement. But first, we'd met up with the cast of *Academy* at a private party he'd planned. Everyone had known but me.

I'd told Martin that I needed a moment to process and skipped upstairs to the hotel room. I had no idea how long I had before he would be up here, but I dialed Maddox before the door even closed behind me.

"Pick up. Pick up. Pick up," I pleaded on the line.

"You've reached the voicemail of Maddox Nelson. Leave a message at the tone."

I cursed violently and then dialed his number again. I had a dozen messages from everyone else in my life— Marley, Lila, my mother, and my dad—congratulating me and asking me so many excited questions about wedding plans. But I couldn't reply to any of them. If they knew ... that meant it had gotten back to Maddox. Shit.

I dialed again. I dialed until he picked up.

"Maddox," I said.

The line was silent on the other end.

"So, you heard?"

Still nothing.

I sank into a chair and brought my hair to my mouth. Old habit that my hairdresser absolutely hated. But I was too anxious to do anything else.

"Please say something."

"You lied to me," he said hoarsely.

"I didn't!"

"You're engaged."

I cringed at the words. "I am, but Maddox, I had no idea it was going to happen."

"You could have said no."

"I wish that were true."

He snorted. I could practically see him sitting in the dark, shaking his head at the absurdity of me.

"I told you it was our last photographed event. I was going to break up with him when I got home and out of the spotlight."

"You'll never be out of the spotlight."

He wasn't wrong. I'd chosen this life, but I'd had every intention of ending it.

"It's not what it looks like. I couldn't end it when he was down on one knee in front of the entire paparazzi. Can you imagine what that would have done to me? Can you understand what it would have done to my career?"

"Ah, there it is. The thing that you actually care about."

"Maddox, I care about you."

And then he started laughing. "Oh, that's ... that's good, Josie. Did you rehearse that?"

"What? No! Maddox, I'm serious. I was going to break up with him. I'm still going to find a way to end this."

"I should have known," he said, losing his mirth. "I should have known that all of this would end in flames. You said exactly what I needed to hear to fall for you all over again. And I fell for it."

"That is not what happened," I argued, my own anger boiling to the surface. "I would never do that to you, Maddox. Everything I said, I meant."

"And somehow, you're engaged to another man."

I opened my mouth to argue with him again, but Martin's voice rang through the penthouse. "Josephine, darling, where have you gone, my love?"

I cringed at those words. "Just one minute," I called out.

"Ah, it sounds like your fiancé is wondering where you've run off to. You should probably go back to him."

"Maddox, please ..."

"Good-bye, Josie. I hope you're both *very* happy."

And then he hung up on me.

I stared down at the phone in shock. Tears threatened to come to my eyes, but I held them back. I couldn't cry right now. I needed to figure out what the hell to do. Maddox wouldn't forgive this. He thought I'd lied all those times I told him I wanted us back together. He thought I'd played him. That I'd been waiting for Martin to get back from filming in Croatia and that I'd dabbled with him until that point. It was so obvious ... and so obviously untrue.

My heart ached as I stared down at the phone. I tried dialing him one more time, but it went instantly to voicemail.

He was gone.

He was really gone.

"My love," Martin slurred, slamming his shoulder into the doorway of the bedroom. He was well past drunk. Everyone at the party had been feeding him alcohol as if he were hooked up to an IV. "What are you doing alone here in the dark? I missed your beautiful presence. I couldn't wait another minute without you."

"Martin, why did you propose to me?" I asked softly. At least I would get the truth from him. He always said exactly what he meant in his inebriated state.

"Whatever do you mean?"

"Was it a publicity stunt? Did your publicist put you up to this?"

His beautiful face scrunched in disbelief. "Of course not. No one suggested it. I want to spend my life with you."

"You do?" I whispered.

He strode across the room and drew me up to him. His arms were so strong and secure around me. His face open and honest. "How could you think otherwise? I love you, Josie. I've loved you for far too long. I was honestly too shy to act on it. You were so intimidating in your strength and endless beauty."

"You were not shy," I said with a strangled laugh.

"I was. I waited too long to make a move on you. I thought you were too good for me."

"Be serious." My face flushed at the words.

"I am," he said, cupping my cheek. "I love you. I want to marry you. I want a life together."

"But the publicity stunts ..."

"Only started after we were together for months. I hadn't planned any of it. I wanted you to be all mine. But when it all came out, I went along with it since it seemed like that was what you wanted."

I blinked in surprise. "Truly?"

I felt wary of him and broken from what had just happened with Maddox. Martin was here. Solid and perfect and saying all the things I'd always wanted to hear from him.

"Forget the publicity. We don't need it." He brushed a kiss on my fingers. "We'll elope. We can do it on Christmas. No one else has to even know."

And I should have said no. I should have walked away and figured out how to be alone if I couldn't have what I really wanted. But I didn't do any of those things. I loved being loved. And I didn't know how to be alone.

So, I said yes.

And by Christmas, Martin Harper was my husband.

21

ATLANTA

PRESENT

I slammed my mother's journal shut with a strangled gasp.

Maddox would be here any moment to pick me up and drive me to Atlanta for my audition. I'd left the set early, unable to look at Martin Harper's stupid face for an extra second. He'd asked if I wanted to go out with the rest of the cast. Nearly three years of marriage had taught me everything I needed to know about the look on his face when he had asked me out tonight. No *way* was I going there again. He'd ruined my relationship with Maddox once. I wasn't letting that happen again.

After having a stilted dinner with my mother and her gentleman caller, Roger, I'd taken up residence on the back porch to read my mother's journal until Maddox got here. I hadn't had much time to read after being on set all day. Plus, I'd been putting off reading past that first summer with my mom and her tangled love triangle with my dad and Edward. I was worried about what I'd find, and it was honestly worse than I'd imagined.

I was supposed to stay the night with my dad tonight. How was I going to face him after reading this?

I stomped inside. I found my mother seated on a divan in the living room. Roger was shaking drinks together in the kitchen.

"You just *gave me up*," I snapped.

Rebecca Charlotte Montgomery hardly looked fazed. "What's that, dear?"

I tossed the precious journal onto the divan next to her. "I don't want to read any more."

"You don't have to if you don't want to."

"How are you so calm?"

She took a sip of her drink. "I lived that life. I told you I had nothing to hide."

Tears pricked my eyes, and I forced them back down. "You chose Edward over Dad and gave up custody of me. You didn't even seem sad about it in the journal."

"I got you every summer."

"I hated that deal," I snarled at her.

"I know, but it was the best that I could do."

"You had this *huge* house and millions of dollars. How in the hell was that the best that you could do?"

"My reasons are in the journal."

"I read it. You had no reasons in there. It was just bull-shit about how you were protecting me."

My mother nodded and set her drink down. She slowly came to her feet and took a step toward me. "That's right."

"Protecting me from *what*?"

And for the first time, my mother looked distant, as if remembering a long-ago pain. "Not what ... who."

I balked at that response. "Who?"

"Honey, everything all right?" Roger asked, stepping tentatively into the bedroom.

That look evaporated from her face, and she preened at the first sight of him. "Absolutely. Just having a chat with my daughter."

"Mother," I said. "Who were you protecting me from?"

She leaned forward and pressed a kiss against my forehead. "I'm proud of how you were raised, dear. Your father did a wonderful job. Isn't that what matters?"

And then she swept past me and toward Roger, never answering my question. It didn't make sense. She and Edward had been happy. Despite the circumstances of how they'd ended up together, I'd never seen a rift between them. Granted, I hadn't seen much of Edward. He had been gone nearly every summer that I was here. But still, I would have been able to tell if she was unhappy, right?

The doorbell rang a moment later. I snatched the journal back up before answering it.

Maddox lifted his Ray-Bans as he took me in. "Everything all right?"

I shook my head. "Just ... my mother."

"Ah," he said, not needing more explanation.

"Maddox Nelson," my mother said behind me.

I rolled my eyes skyward.

Maddox just smiled. "Hello, Mrs. Montgomery."

"Rebecca, please. Do take care of my daughter this weekend."

"I certainly intend to."

My mother's gaze shifted back to me. She looked torn for a whole second before a smile hit her features again. "Read the rest of the journal, Josephine."

I waved it at her. "Yeah, I guess I will."

Then, I grabbed my suitcase, shouldered my purse, and followed Maddox out to his Jeep.

"So, what's going on with you two now?" he asked as he pulled out of Savannah and headed north, toward Atlanta.

I huffed. "This damn journal. I thought it would bring us together, but all it does is make me furious with her."

"What happened now?"

"She chose Edward and gave me up. She didn't even have remorse. She said she did it to protect me from someone but won't say who."

"Edward?"

I shrugged. "I mean, that's what the gossipers would have me believe. She *murdered* him," I said, waggling my fingers at him. "Easier to think she did something horrible like that than to believe he overdosed."

"But you don't believe it anymore?"

"I don't know what I believe," I answered honestly.

"So, why did she choose Edward? Did you find that out?"

I sighed and slumped forward. It felt too close to reality to say the words out loud. "Uh, Dad wouldn't take her back."

Maddox cleared his throat. "I see."

"Yeah. So ... so she married Edward and gave up custody of me." I met his gaze. "If she couldn't have the man she loved, then she could at least try to be happy."

"Ah."

"I might have more in common with my mother than I knew. After all, I married Martin, right?"

"I wasn't going to say that, Jos. That was a long time ago."

"I know," I whispered. "But I still regret how it all happened."

He reached over and laced our fingers together. "We're not repeating your mother's history."

"Yeah. It just ... there are so many what-ifs in my head about us. I don't want to repeat our *own* history. Let alone my mother's."

"You're not planning to marry Martin again, are you?" he asked with a tilt to his lips.

"No!" I gasped, swatting at him.

"Then, I think we're safe on that front."

I laughed. "You've got jokes."

"Hey, I saw him kissing you on set."

"Yeah, and I went apoplectic and screamed at him."

Maddox smirked. "Oh, I saw."

"Felt good?"

He chuckled. "Maybe a little."

"I'm still amazed you're working on this movie."

"Yeah, well, there's one thing you haven't considered."

"What's that?"

He took my hand and brought it to his lips. "*You're* in the movie."

We arrived in Atlanta four hours later. My stomach was in knots as my dad answered the door. He looked the same as ever—unruly hair as dark as night with week-old scruff. He was dressed in a paint-splattered T-shirt and shorts he'd had my entire life.

"You made it," he said, pulling the door open for the pair of us. "I'm glad you're here."

"Hey, Dad." I threw my arms around him, squeezing the life out of him.

"Whoa there, Josie. It's good to see you too."

I laughed and released him. "Remember Maddox?"

"Nice to see you again, sir," he said, holding his hand out.

My dad shook his hand. "Heard a lot about you, but I haven't seen you since you were about fifteen. You've grown up."

Maddox ran a hand through his curls. "A little, yeah."

"Well, let's get you inside."

Dad took my suitcase out of my hand and carried it to my old room. It was no longer a place for me. More like an art room that happened to have a queen bed in it.

"Sorry about the mess," he said, kicking at a tube of paint on the ground. "This room has the best light."

"It doesn't matter to me," I assured him.

I'd tried to get Dad to move into something nicer when I got *Academy* money, but he was happy, living here. We'd bought the place, so he no longer had to rent, but he didn't want anything bigger or better. That was all me. So, I'd given up on that and let him live the life he loved. He had the studio, which had taken off in the last couple of years, and I was so proud of him.

"You like beer?" my dad asked Maddox.

He laughed. "Yes, sir."

"Ah, drop the *sir* bit. You can call me Charles."

Maddox nodded and followed him into the kitchen. We were only here one night. Tomorrow, we'd be staying with Lila and Cole, but I couldn't come into Atlanta without paying my dad a visit.

I changed into something more comfortable and found my dad and Maddox in front of an easel, holding beers and discussing the merits of the project. I completely disappeared as Maddox suggested some technique and my dad's eyes got wide and excited as he learned that Maddox was also an artist.

"You told me he did visual effects," my dad accused.

I laughed. "He does."

"Art is my first passion though," Maddox said. "I sketch a lot with charcoals or graphite when I need to clear my head or visualize what I want to create on the computer."

"Oh no, I'm going to have to listen to nerdy art-boy talk all night, aren't I?"

My dad beamed. "As if you're not used to it."

I was. And watching my father not just accept Maddox, but also immediately love him made my heart bloom. I hadn't realized how similar they were until that moment as they ignored me and focused on the artwork.

All thoughts of bringing up my mother's journal vanished. I'd made the same choice as my mother. I'd chosen the rich guy … twice. Instead of the artist who adored me. I wouldn't make that same mistake again.

22

ATLANTA
PRESENT

I woke at the break of dawn to prepare for my audition. I'd thought I'd be more nervous, considering how much I wanted this part, but I felt ready. As if I'd been waiting my entire life for this. Maddox offered to drive me to the studio, which I considered denying, but I could see he was just as excited for me, so I let him.

Two hours later, it was all over. I was giddy as I traipsed out of the studio toward Maddox's Jeep. He stepped out of the truck and grinned as I skipped toward him. I didn't even think; I flung my arms around his neck and kissed him.

He laughed as he twirled me in place. "So, I'm guessing the audition went okay?" he asked as he set me back on my feet.

"Glorious. I was *made* for this role, Maddox."

He followed me around to the side of the truck and opened my door for me. "That good?"

"Even better. They have a few more auditions to get

through, but the casting director basically said I had it in the bag."

"That's incredible," he said when he got in on the driver's side.

I sagged backward. "I've worked so hard to get to this point. I can't wait for *Academy* to be over, so I can step into this new role."

"All the possibilities."

"And you," I said, turning his face toward me.

"What about me?"

"I want this to work this time, Maddox."

He drew my face toward his. Our lips sealed together. The promises neither of us had been able to utter all those years before. The ones we'd hoped for and broken time and time again. It was all spread before us on a platter.

"Maybe we should get a room tonight," I said baldly.

He grinned. "Now who can't keep their hands to themselves?"

I groaned as he pulled away and started the car. "Not fair."

And despite the levity, I could see the shadows of fear in his irises. We'd been here before, and as wonderful as it was, there was always the fear that it wouldn't work out. That I'd go back to LA and forget him. I refused to let that happen this time.

"Fine. What's the plan anyway?" I said with a pout.

"We're meeting Lila, Cole, and Marley for lunch at Centennial."

"That's a choice," I said with a laugh.

Centennial Olympic Park was at the heart of downtown Atlanta with water shooting out of the iconic rings that kids ran through all summer. It was also tourist central and not really a place we'd casually go to when there were a million other places to do lunch.

He shrugged. "I haven't been in years."

"All right. Are we going to eat in the CNN Center, like real tourists? Or walk down Peachtree?"

"Which Peachtree?" he asked with a laugh. "They still confuse me."

"Oh, poor thing. You really are a tourist."

Sometimes, I forgot that I'd grown up in Atlanta and not Savannah. The coastal city had always felt more like home even though I'd spent nine months out of the year in the ATL until my eighteenth birthday.

Maddox squeezed my hand and drove through the weekend Atlanta traffic, finding parking near the giant Ferris wheel, which lit up the streets at night. I took his hand as we headed into the park and found Cole, Lila, and Marley already seated at a table, eating a huge array of food from The Varsity.

"There are my girls," I said, crushing my two best friends to me. "I missed your faces."

"How'd it go?" Lila asked.

"Excellent!"

"You got the part?" Marley asked.

"Well, I won't know for a few weeks, but I think I have it in the bag." I hugged Cole next. "Hey, handsome."

"Hey, Josie. We didn't know what you wanted. So, we got a bit of everything."

I realized the spread before us was way too much food

for just the three of them. "Thanks. There's a reason you're my favorite."

Cole smirked. "The food is the reason?"

I took the seat next to Lila, and Maddox sat next to me. "Nah, probably because I was there when the two of you started. I was responsible for those viral pictures of y'all at the UGA game," I said, putting my hand to my chest. "I had to be right."

Lila smacked me. "Shush you," she said with a laugh.

Cole put a possessive arm around her shoulders. "Hey, we like her to be right, don't we, Sunflower?"

Marley gagged. "You should be glad Derek isn't here. He'd be making fun of y'all so bad."

"Where is the lovely Derek Ballentine?" I asked.

"Work. He said he'd meet up with us later," Mars said. She looked between me and her brother. "And you two? Holding hands?"

Lila squealed. She flipped her blonde hair off of her shoulders and leaned forward. "Is it official? Are y'all back together?"

Maddox and I shared a glance. We hadn't defined anything, but I couldn't deny that I wanted that.

"Leave them be," Cole said, tugging his girlfriend back to him.

"Well?" Mars asked her brother. "I can be annoying and persistent. I don't have my other half telling me to be less annoying."

I snorted. "Derek would encourage it."

Marley grinned. "True."

Maddox's gaze swept back to mine. "Yeah, I guess we are."

My body melted at those words. It had taken cajoling from his sister for him to even admit it. But fuck, what else were we doing? I wasn't just fucking around here. I wanted this. I'd made myself clear. It was him that I'd thought I'd have to convince.

"Oh good," I said, planting a kiss on him. "That clears that up."

Maddox rolled his eyes at me and draped an arm around me. "You dragged me out here just to get me to admit it."

Marley snorted. "As if you needed to be convinced. You've been obsessed with her since you were fifteen."

Maddox threw a French fry at his sister. "Jerk."

She tossed one back. "Bitch."

We all dissolved into laughter as the twins sniped at each other. It all felt so fucking *normal*. I couldn't be happier. I'd missed having Lila around. She completed our trifecta. And Maddox here with me was the best of it all.

When we finished eating our lunch, we trashed the rest of the food and headed south, toward Lila and Cole's job. Lila was a physical therapist, and Cole was in recruiting, both for the Falcons football team. Their joint love of football had always been a huge part of their relationship, and now that they were working for the same team, it was even better.

"Work?" I groaned.

"Don't you want to see the behind-the-scenes at the stadium?" Maddox asked.

I shot him a skeptical look. "Since when do you care about football?"

He shrugged. "Never."

I laughed. That was the damn truth. But I was too happy, having everyone I loved in one place, that I didn't even care. I skipped ahead, linking arms with my two best friends and leaving the boys in the dust.

"We missed you last weekend," I told Lila.

She sighed. "Yeah. I wish I could have come into town."

"Derek needed the best-friend time too," Marley said softly.

Lila shot her a look. "I know."

I felt for her. It was as if she and Ash were divorced and had to split the kids. Derek was Ash's best friend and Marley's husband. So, Lila only got her half the time. With me in Savannah, too, it had to be killing her.

Lila looked over her shoulder at Cole, as if to make sure he wasn't in hearing distance before asking softly, "How's he doing?"

Marley and I exchanged a glance. By unspoken agreement, we never mentioned Ash in front of Lila or Lila in front of Ash. Well, I did to fuck with him, but that was just for fun.

"He's doing okay, you know?" I told her just as softly.

"Much better," Marley added.

"Not drowning himself anymore?"

Marley shook her head. "He's seeing someone."

Her head snapped up with wide eyes. "Really?"

I rolled my eyes. "Well, if you heard it from her lips, she'd say they're not together."

"Why not?" Lila asked in a half-whisper.

"You know why," Marley said.

She bit her lip. "Yeah. Probably still my fault."

"Your friend *James* is going to be fine," I told her confidently. "I promise. You can't keep blaming yourself. You made your choice, right?"

"A hundred percent," she said without even a thought.

Two years ago, she would have agonized over her decision. But she chose Cole. It was definitely Cole. No matter how it had hurt her over the years to get there.

"Then, be happy he's moving on and revel in your very handsome boyfriend."

Lila's smile went brilliant. The fallout with Ash Talmadge sliding off of her shoulders as easily as it had come back to her. "You're right. Thanks for letting me know."

We squeezed her tighter to us and then reached the employee entrance to the Mercedes-Benz Stadium. Lila and Cole swiped their badges, and we followed them inside. After a quick tour of the employee facilities, Cole showed us where the football players ran out.

I took Maddox's hand again as Cole led Lila out first. My jaw dropped when I realized what was happening. The field was *full* of sunflowers. As if Cole Davis had plucked an entire field of sunflowers to arrange them in a beautiful display.

"Oh my God," I gasped at the same time as Marley.

Lila's hands went to her mouth as Cole took her hand and drew her out to the center of the field.

"Delilah Grace Greer, I've loved you my entire life," Cole said, dropping to a knee and withdrawing a little blue box from his pocket. "You're the best thing that has ever happened to me. I've lived a lifetime knowing that one day you'd be mine. And I want everything with you. I want you to be my wife and take my name and have my children."

Lila sniffled as tears came to her eyes. "Oh, Cole."

"I love you with all of my heart. Make me the happiest man alive. Marry me, Sunflower."

She nodded. "Yes, yes, yes. Of course I'll marry you."

He slid the ring on her finger and effortlessly lifted her off of her feet. It was like when he'd jumped the hedges to claim her lips in college. They'd come a long way since that day, and no one deserved it more.

"You knew," I accused Maddox.

He looked at me sheepishly. "Maybe."

"You knew?" Marley gasped. "You didn't tell us?!"

"Cole called after we said we were coming into town. I knew she'd want y'all here."

"Thank you," I said, kissing him before running after my best friend and all but tackling her. "Let me see that ring!"

Lila laughed to cover the tears streaming down her cheeks. She held her hand out to reveal a perfectly Lila ring. A giant round diamond with a small diamond halo and a second halo that almost made the ring look like a sunflower.

"I love it."

"It's perfect!" Marley said, tugging her into a hug.

I nudged Cole and winked. "You did good."

His smile was brilliant. "It's about damn time."

I snorted. "I wasn't going to say it."

"Someone had to!" Marley said. "I never thought I'd be married before y'all."

"You eloped!" Lila accused. But her eyes were locked on the ring. She turned back to her fiancé and pressed her lips to his. "It's perfect."

"Good."

"We have a lot to plan."

"A small wedding," he promised with a gleam in his eyes.

"Maybe we shouldn't send out invitations," she joked.

He grinned wider. "I'll get better security."

She dissolved into laughter and fell back into his arms. I'd never been happier for her.

Maddox wrapped an arm around my waist and kissed my temple. "They deserve this," he said softly.

"I'm still mad you didn't tell me."

He just laughed and kissed me, silencing all of my complaints. I was here with him, and everything in the world suddenly made sense.

23

ATLANTA
PRESENT

To celebrate Lila's engagement, we all got dolled up and went to a fancy bar in Buckhead. Even Derek joined us. I could see doubt in Lila's eyes about telling him, knowing Ash was his best friend, but she was too excited to keep it quiet.

I glanced at Derek as Lila dragged Cole out onto the dance floor. "So ..."

"I'm not telling him," he said before I could say anything else.

"Someone is going to have to tell him," Marley said. "He can't find out some other way."

"He doesn't need to know," Derek argued.

"I'm with Derek," Maddox said. "Why the fuck should it matter? He's enamored with Amelia anyway."

"Yeah, except ... it matters," I said.

Derek sighed. "Yeah, it matters, but we can't do it yet."

"Why not?" I asked.

Marley rolled her eyes. "They're going sailing to see Derek's cousins at the end of the month."

Derek grimaced. "Forgive me for wanting him to enjoy a vacation. We've had this trip planned for ages. He'll bail if he finds out before then."

"Then, after that trip," Marley said.

"Yeah. Yeah, I'll tell him after the trip," Derek said.

We all nodded. Plotting how to tell Ash Talmadge the news felt disgusting, but in some way, we all cared about him. Lila cared about him. I even cared about the bastard. And I could admit that I didn't want to see him crawl back into the hole he'd fallen into when he and Lila ended.

With our clandestine agreement finalized, Derek pulled Marley out onto the dance floor.

"Do you think this is a good idea?" Maddox asked.

"I have no idea. But I can't exactly ask Lila what she thinks."

"No. I remember when we lived together when she was in PT school," he said, his eyes going distant. "She and Ash were dating, and look, I know she loved him, but he was *obsessed* with her. It was unhealthy. Not that I could say that to her."

"She wouldn't have heard you. Trust me. I *did* say that."

"It's probably better he finds out right away. Otherwise, he's going to do something stupid."

I shrugged. "I bet he does something stupid either way."

"Do you think that's why Cole waited this long?"

"Nah. Cole Davis doesn't give a shit what Ash thinks. Lila wanted to wait. She and Cole were endgame. The wedding part didn't matter to her."

"Yeah, you're probably right."

"I'm always right," I said, leaning up onto my toes to kiss him. "Like about us."

He laughed. "Nice topic change there."

"Hey, you're the one who said we were together."

"I did," he said, sliding his hands around me. "I can't seem to fight you. Even when I tried all those years, I really failed. I always wanted to be exactly where I am. How can I give you up when you're right here in front of me?"

"Please don't give me up," I whispered. "Especially when I make you dance with me."

I grabbed his hand and pulled him toward the dance floor and our friends. He groaned behind me. He hated dancing and going out and peopling, but he was here with me, celebrating Lila. Even if it was one dance, it felt so right.

Despite Maddox always refusing to dance with me, he sure had rhythm. I never would have guessed it as he grasped my hips in his hands and swayed side to side to the gyrating music.

"Fuck, Josie," he whispered against my ear. "I've been keeping my hands to myself all week." He jerked my hips back against his. I bit back a groan. "Now, you're here ..."

I knew exactly what he meant. I'd teased him that he couldn't keep his hands to himself this long. And we'd slept in the same bed last night with my back pressed against his chest, his strong hands holding me in place against him. I'd wanted to go further, but we'd been in my dad's house. Personally, I knew how thin the walls were, and that was the last thing I wanted my dad to hear. Plus, when we rushed into things, they found a way of falling apart.

But now that he'd said he was mine, I had no chill left. I'd booked a hotel, so Lila and Cole could have the house to themselves to celebrate, and I was already prepared to leave. To get up to that fancy suite and fall into his arms. It had been too damn long.

I wrapped my arms around his neck, and then I pulled his mouth down to mine. He kissed me with an urgency that was unparalleled. From years of tension built between us. I wanted to fall down the rabbit hole and never come up from Wonderland.

But it would be hours later before we could reasonably leave.

"I want you *now*," I said into his ear.

"I know."

"Right now," I said more urgently.

I winked at him, and he shook his head at me with a laugh.

"Fuck, how do you do this to me?"

Then he grabbed my hand and pulled me off of the dance floor. I had no idea where we were going, and I didn't care. But I was shocked when he pushed me into the restroom, decisively locking the door behind us.

"What—"

But my words were cut off by Maddox pushing me back against the sink. His fingers went up into my hair, crushing our lips together.

"We'll have to be quick," he said. His hands roamed down to the hem of my dress, hiking it up around my stomach.

K.A. LINDE

I reached eagerly for the button on his jeans. "This is so unlike you."

"I've waited too damn long for you. I'll take my time later tonight. Right now, I fucking need you."

He hoisted me up onto the sink.

"Yes," I gasped.

My hand closed around his cock, and he released a heavy breath.

"Fucking hell," he groaned.

I stroked him up and down as his fingers moved my thong to the side and began to massage my sensitive skin. When he found the bud of my clit, I shuddered. I was already wet. With how things had been building between us, I didn't need any foreplay.

"Jesus," he groaned against my lips. "You're so wet."

"Fuck me," I begged.

He positioned my hips for better access and then lined up our bodies. He slid in with no resistance, and I nearly blacked out. It had been so fucking long.

"Oh my God," I said on a breath.

"Fuck yes," he said.

Then, our words went incoherent as he withdrew and slammed back into me. I tried to brace myself against the sink as he pounded into me, but I had no control of the situation. Someone was banging on the restroom door, yelling at us to hurry up. But I couldn't give a single shit.

I hadn't even considered what would happen if someone recognized me. It would be shitty if this got back to the press. Risky, but worth it as far as I was concerned.

"Jos," he ground out. "I'm close."

"So fucking close," I agreed. "Make me come."

He groaned, picking up the pace. Sweat beaded on my brow from the Atlanta summer and the exertion. I saw stars as my orgasm went from zero to a hundred. As if he'd flipped on a light switch.

I muffled my cry as it hit me in a wave. He grunted and tightened his grip on my hips hard enough to bruise as he came inside of me.

We both stilled, breathing hard. Our eyes locked, and I saw nothing but love in those dark irises. He would find nothing but that mirrored in my own green orbs. I wanted to tell him. It might have been reckless, but I wouldn't change it for the world.

But then he withdrew, and the moment broke.

I dropped down onto my heels. The banging on the door intensified.

Maddox chuckled. "Guess there's a line."

"Whoops."

We cleaned up, and I ducked my head as we left, hoping no one noticed who I was. We made a mini walk of shame as we headed back to our friends. Lila gave me a very knowing look and giggled.

She gestured to my lips. "You've got a little ..." She wiped away the lipstick that must have been smudged.

"Thanks," I said with a laugh.

"Good thing Marley is getting drinks."

"Well, don't tell her it was the best of my life then."

Lila put her hand out, and we high-fived. Then, I fell back into Maddox's arms.

"Who knew you were so dirty?" I said, drawing his mouth down to mine.

"Guess you bring it out in me." He brushed his nose along my earlobe. "Didn't exactly hear you complaining."

"Oh, no. No complaints from me."

"Good, because I think we're going to need to do that a couple times tonight."

I smirked up at him. "You read my mind."

Derek and Marley returned a minute later with a round of champagne. Everyone held their glasses aloft and toasted Cole and Lila. I was happy that my friends were happy, but I was glad that I was finally getting my own happily ever after.

PART IV

PART IV

24

SAVANNAH

MARCH 11, 2013

If one more person spoke to me, I was going to combust. Everyone thought that since Martin and I had gotten married less than three months earlier, I wanted to be with him all the time.

We'd come back to Atlanta after our spontaneous Bora Bora honeymoon, and suddenly, my trailer had disappeared. I'd fought tooth and nail for my own *fucking* space. I was the star of the show after all. Then, someone had even written Josephine *Harper* on all of my scripts and paperwork. I'd blown a gasket. I was married. I wasn't a *different person*. And I certainly wasn't changing my name. The internalized misogyny was driving me batshit crazy.

I slammed the door on my brand-new Josephine Reynolds trailer. Martin had laughed on set when I had to correct another person about my name. He'd *laughed*. Even though he knew I was pissed. I'd had enough of him today.

We'd had a beautiful wedding and a dream honeymoon. It hadn't been what I'd planned, but I'd enjoyed every minute of it. Now that reality was crashing back in, it was a whole new world.

I snatched my phone off of the charger and slouched back into the couch, but then I stilled when I saw the missed call.

"Maddox?" I whispered in shock.

I hadn't heard a single thing from him since he'd hung up on me before Christmas. Not that I blamed him. He was right. I shouldn't have started anything with him before breaking it off with Martin, and it was terrible optics that I'd gotten engaged. I was in the wrong. Not that he'd let me get that out. Now, I was married. Why the hell would he reach out?

But I didn't stop and think before dialing him back.

He answered almost instantly. "Josie."

I stilled. He sounded ... sad. Like he'd been crying.

"Maddox, are you okay? I got your missed call."

"Gramps is dead."

I gasped. My hand went to my mouth, and tears came to my eyes. Gramps hadn't been doing well the last couple years. He'd been in a home for dementia, but I hadn't heard that it was this bad.

"Oh my God, Maddox, I'm so sorry. He was a wonderful man. I loved him too."

"I don't know why I called you," he admitted.

"Because ... I'm your person," I whispered.

He sighed. "Yeah. I don't know. Mars is probably going to call you too. I could have let her."

"I'm glad you didn't."

"Yeah," he said, sounding utterly dejected. "I didn't

know what else to do. I have a fucking girlfriend, and the first thing I did when I found out was call you."

I winced at the word *girlfriend*. I had no right. None at all. But I couldn't stop the feeling of disgust when I heard it.

"It's okay. You're allowed to feel how you feel."

"I don't know how I feel."

"Heartbroken," I whispered.

"Fuck, I should go."

"Hey," I said softly, consolingly. "Do you need me to come into town? I'm in Atlanta. I could drive down there."

"Don't you have work?"

"Gramps was family. I can get out of it."

"No, you should stay."

"Maddox," I growled. "You called me for a reason."

"Yeah ... yeah." He sighed. "Yeah, okay."

"I'll be there in four hours."

I wasted no time, letting everyone know that I had to leave. Production looked pissed, but when I told them I had a death in the family, there was nothing they could say.

"Babe," Martin said. "Do you want me to come with you?"

"Uh, no. You know, you should stay here. I need to deal with this."

Martin touched my arm. I could see that he didn't really want to drive down to Savannah for this, but he was being supportive. So, I relented and let him pull me into a quick hug.

"I'll text you when I get there," I promised my husband.

He pressed a kiss to my lips and then let me go. Little did he know.

A twinge of regret ran through me. I could have told him the truth. I could have let him come with me. I could have done a million things, but I didn't. I got into my new black Mercedes and drove the four hours to Savannah.

Maddox needed me.

Lila opened the door when I arrived. She and Maddox had been living together since August when she started at physical therapy school. Two dogs barked and ran in circles when they saw me standing in the doorway.

Maddox's shih tzu, Walt, nipped at my ankles while Lila's puppy, Sunny, had the zoomies. I dropped down to pet and quiet them both before standing up again before my friend and pulling her into a hug.

"Hey," I said. "How are you doing?"

"Sad. Maddox hasn't come out of his room. I talked to Mars. She's flying down for the funeral."

"Good."

I stepped inside and found Ash Talmadge standing there. It felt like an intrusion. He and Lila had started dating again in December. I wanted to be happy for her, but I'd never forgiven him for hurting her. I was crazy loyal to my friends even if I let myself get hurt.

"James," I said dryly.

"Josephine," he threw back.

"Be nice," Lila said with a sad smile as she slid into his arms.

"I'm always nice." Ash brushed a kiss into her hair. He looked ... besotted. Like he'd won the lottery to have her in his life again. He'd better fucking act like it forever because he'd never get this chance again as far as I was concerned.

"I'm going to go see Maddox."

Lila bit her lip. "Does ... Martin know you're here?"

"Yeah."

"Does he know why?"

"A death in the family," I offered.

Lila hugged me again. "Be careful," she whispered.

I didn't need the warning. I knew why I was here. I didn't have any illusion that Maddox and I would reconcile. Not after I'd married someone else.

I knocked twice on Maddox's door and then stepped into the darkened room. "Hey."

Maddox was on his back on the bed. He was shirtless, in nothing but boxers, as he stared blankly up at the ceiling. "Hey."

I kicked off my shoes and dropped my jacket. "How are you doing?"

"The same as I was four hours ago."

"Can I ..." I gestured to the bed.

His eyes slid to mine then. They were red-rimmed. He and Gramps had always been close. Gramps had supported his art, even when Gran was a little too hard on him for not caring about academics. Gramps had encouraged him to get the SCAD scholarship. He'd been there through all the ups and downs. I couldn't imagine how Maddox felt to lose him.

When he didn't say no, I slipped onto the bed next to

him. I reached out and took his hand in mine. He sighed and then laced our fingers together. His eyes closed at the contact, and I tried to slow my heart rate. I was here for him. This wasn't sexual. I wasn't going to do anything stupid. But sometimes, it was really fucking hard to suppress the way I felt about him.

"I'm glad you're here," he finally said.

I scooted closer until our shoulders were touching. My eyes were still on his face. "I'm glad you let me come."

Then, he shifted his arm out to the side and offered me the space against his side. I scooted in, resting my head against his chest, my arm draping across his waist. His fingers moved through my dark hair.

I had no idea how long we lay like that. Just holding each other through the worst of the pain. At some point, I made him get up and eat something. Then, we returned to his bedroom, wrapped up like a cocoon under the covers.

At some point, he rolled me over and pulled my back to his chest. I fit against him as if I'd been made for it. His arms were around my body, holding me tight. Even though what had happened was terrible, I felt closer to him than ever. At some point in the night, he started whispering to me, telling me all the stories he could remember about Gramps.

We must have fallen asleep in each other's arms because I woke the next morning to sunlight streaming in through the windows. Maddox still held me tight to his chest.

An urgent knock on the bedroom door made him jerk upright. "What?"

"Maddox, Teena is at the door," Lila said.

"Fuck," Maddox said, scrambling out of bed.

My eyes were wide as I realized who Teena must be—the girlfriend. Not good.

His eyes jerked to mine. "I ..."

"You don't have to explain," I said quickly. "Go see her."

He nodded, tugged on shorts and a T-shirt, and hurried out of the room. I made sure to grab anything I'd left in his room and dashed across the hall into the bathroom. I felt fifteen again, sneaking around to hide out from parents. Though Maddox and I had done nothing wrong, it certainly wasn't platonic and hadn't been in years.

It was twenty minutes later when Maddox knocked on the bathroom door. "Jos?"

I cracked the door. "Your girlfriend?"

He nodded, hanging his head. "I shouldn't have told you to come here."

"Yeah," I whispered.

"Besides my girlfriend ... you're married."

"I know."

"I shouldn't want to see you anymore."

Shouldn't wasn't *don't*, and we both knew it.

Our eyes finally met. I could see the pain was still there. Maybe it would always be there. Gramps was more a father to him than the dad he'd never met. But something had lessened since I'd shown up, and I couldn't regret driving down here to see him if that was true.

"You should ... you should probably go."

"But the funeral."

He swallowed, and then his eyes hardened. "I don't think you should come to the funeral."

My stomach dropped. Gramps had helped raise me too. I'd stayed at their house over the years almost as much as my mother's. It hurt to think I couldn't be there. But if I'd been honest with Martin from the start ... Maddox and I could have been together right now, and there would have been no explanations. These were the consequences of my own actions.

I swiped at the tear that streaked down my cheek. "Okay. If that's what you want."

He opened his mouth like he was going to deny it but then snapped it shut.

I stepped forward and drew him into a hug. After a second, he relented and wrapped his arms around me. I knew this was good-bye. And as much as I hated saying it, I was lucky to even get this moment with him.

We lived two different lives. I couldn't have it both ways.

I pressed a kiss to his cheek. "I'll always be here if you need me."

Then, I walked out the door and drove back to Atlanta.

25

NEW YORK CITY

JULY 23, 2015

"I can't believe you insisted that I work with you," Amelia said.

"Hey, I'm always here to help out hometown girls."

I'd run into Amelia Ballentine when I was being fitted for a Teen Choice Award the previous year. I had no idea that she worked for Cunningham Couture after graduating from Parsons. When we'd discovered our Savannah connection, we'd become fast friends. With the Emmys coming up in a few short weeks, I'd reached back out to have her dress me. I was up for Best Actress, and I wanted something innovative and incredible.

"Sometimes, I think about going back," she admitted.

I arched an eyebrow at her in the mirror as she pinned my dress for alterations. "Really? To Savannah? What would you do there?"

"I don't know. Open up my own boutique."

"And give up high fashion?"

She shrugged. "It's just a thought. I hate being away

from home, especially since my brother is back in Savannah."

My expression soured. Derek and Marley were currently on the outs after he'd been a total ass when they were at Harvard. As much as I liked him for her, they were a toxic mess. They needed to grow up and out of it. Until then, I'd continue to dislike him.

"I know. I know," Amelia said with a laugh, standing to survey her handiwork. "He was a jerk to Marley. But he's dating someone new now, and she's *awful*. I need to be there to guide him away from that train wreck. I'd *much* prefer Marley. Trust me."

I laughed. "Wouldn't we all?"

"Well, what do you think?" Amelia asked. "It fits you like a glove."

"You're a genius."

The dress was phenomenal. As green as my eyes and the perfect silk masterpiece. I loved every inch of it.

"I can't wait to see you on the red carpet in it. If you don't mind me saying, Martin Harper is going to realize how much of an idiot he is."

I laughed. "I don't mind that at all."

Martin and I were in the middle of a mutual but generally messy divorce. It was a long time coming, if I was honest. In fact, all of it should be final any day now. I was just waiting for him to sign his stupid name on the paperwork.

"And you know how I feel about him," Amelia said with a wink.

"Ah yes, didn't we all grow up loving him?"

I had no malice toward Martin. He'd been the man of

my dreams before I really knew him. I couldn't blame him for not living up to the hype. But I was going to split our assets fifty-fifty and get the fuck out as fast as I could. We still had to work together on *Academy*, but it couldn't be worse than filming this last season in the midst of our divorce.

"What about you?"

"What about me?" Amelia asked, gesturing for me to step out of the dress.

"Any lucky man for you?"

She shook her head. "Nah. I was dating a guy for a while who helped me get this job, but he was ... not a good guy. Anyway, he's engaged to someone else now."

"And no new men in your life?"

"I've gone on dates, but they're all so ... northern."

I cackled at that assessment as I pulled my dress back on. "You want a Southern gentleman?"

"I can't help but love them." She winked at me.

"Someone like ... Ash Talmadge?" I guessed. She'd mentioned him to me a few times over the last couple years, and she knew exactly what I thought about him. But in those conversations, I could gather exactly what *she* thought about him.

She startled anyway. "Um ... uh ..."

"It's all right. He's single right now, isn't he?"

Lila was back with Cole, which I personally thought was good for her. Not that it stopped her from swinging between the boys like a pendulum.

"He ... is," Amelia admitted. "But I've known him my whole life, he's my brother's best friend, and ... I don't know if he'll really ever get over her."

K.A. LINDE

That I did know.

"Good. You can do better," I said, and she laughed.

"I like the way you make things seem so simple." Amelia gathered up the dress. "I should have this ready for you in a week or two. In time for your show."

"Perfect. Let's get lunch or something when I'm back in town."

"Done."

I hugged Amelia and headed back out onto the New York City streets. I pulled my phone out of my bag and was surprised to find a missed call from my attorney. I listened to the voicemail she'd left, which brought me to a standstill in the middle of the busy street.

I was a free woman. Martin had signed the paperwork. The divorce was final.

"Oh my God," I said, breathing a sigh of relief.

I hadn't considered that I was out in public and someone would likely recognize me. I was too ecstatic to be free again that I did a little twirl in the middle of the street.

And despite all the reasons not to, the first person I called was Maddox. We hadn't spoken in years. Not since I'd driven out to Savannah for him after Gramps died. But still, I wanted to hear his voice even if I had no expectation that he'd answer.

"Josie?" he said softly on the other line.

My body relaxed at the sound of his voice. "Hey, Maddox."

"Everything all right?"

"Fine," I said. "Just fine actually."

"Uh, okay. I thought ..." He trailed off. "I guess it doesn't matter. Why are you calling?"

"Right this minute, I am officially divorced."

There was silence on the other end. Maybe he hadn't heard me?

"Maddox, I'm a free woman."

"Congratulations, I guess," he said.

"It is a big congratulations."

"I'd heard that it was happening. I wasn't sure if you were happy."

"Joyous. I'm nominated for an Emmy, I'm on a New York City street, and the world is my oyster."

"You're in New York?" he nearly choked out.

"Yep! I was getting fitted for my Emmy dress."

Another long pause before he said, "I'm in New York."

"Shut up," I said before I could stop myself.

He chuckled. "Yeah, I'm working on a movie."

I'd heard that Maddox had moved on from Pixar after winning an Oscar for an animated film and then went right into CGI, winning a second Oscar for his visual effects in a superhero film the next year. I had expected nothing less from his brilliance and was not at all jealous ...

"That seems fitting."

"Look, I'm here until late, but ... do you want to get a drink later to celebrate?"

My insides twisted with excitement. "I would love that."

"I'll text you when I'm done."

"Sounds good."

I said my good-byes and hung up. I had the rest of the

day in New York City before I saw Maddox, and I knew exactly what I needed to do—shop.

It was nearly midnight when I stepped into Club 360, the rooftop bar on top of Percy Tower. I was staying at the hotel, and Maddox had agreed to meet me there. It was a random Thursday night in July, but still, the place was packed. I was glad that I'd called ahead to arrange a VIP booth. Maddox hated this many people on a good day.

I followed a bouncer to my booth and ordered drinks when Maddox showed up.

"You got a booth," he said with surprise.

"I didn't think you'd be okay with this many people."

"That is ... correct."

I stood, and he pulled me into a hug. I hadn't seen him in years. His hair was cut ridiculously short, even for him. No sign of his curls at all. He was in a plain gray T-shirt and jeans, and still, he was the most handsome person in the room.

"God, I missed you," he breathed against my hair.

"Same."

I didn't want to let him go. I wanted to live in this moment forever with his arms around me and his face in my hair and the world disappearing. But I couldn't do that. I might be divorced, but I was far from ready to jump back into anything. Even if Maddox wanted that, which I had many, *many* doubts about.

Finally, I stepped back, and he took the seat opposite me. Our drinks came a minute later. I'd gotten him a beer, which he accepted, while I had a sidecar. I'd felt nostalgic as I ordered it.

Maddox held his drink aloft. "To your divorce."

I clinked my glass against his sweating beer bottle. "To freedom."

We each took a sip and leaned back in our seats. It wasn't uncomfortable to be here with him despite the years apart. It never had been with Maddox. Even when he used to go nonverbal at my approach as kids, it had still been easy.

"So, what's next?"

We chatted about mindless things for an hour. Just two friends catching up. He told me about his work on his current movie. I told him that I was grateful for the break in filming for *Academy*. He mentioned a new visual effects setup that he was working on, but he felt he was still years away from being able to implement.

We talked about everything, except us and our relationships.

At two in the morning, Maddox couldn't hold back his yawn. "Fuck, sorry. I am not bored by our conversation. I had to be up at five yesterday, and I have an early start tomorrow."

"They're working you to the bone."

"You have no idea. It's been exhausting."

"But professionally satisfying?"

"Definitely. They're always willing to take it to the next level, and I'm always eager to do the same."

"Well, maybe we should head out. It's already two. We don't have to close the bar down."

"But you're leaving tomorrow," he pointed out. I nodded. "Then, we should stay."

I laughed. "You're going to be cursing me in the morning."

His eyes tracked over my face for a second and then hastily away. As if to say that wasn't what he wanted to be doing to me in the morning.

My face flushed, and I set my third empty drink on the table. I didn't need a fourth or else we'd end up in my hotel room downstairs. I was sure there was a reason that relationships hadn't come up, and I didn't want to do anything to hurt him.

He yawned wide again. "Sorry. Sorry."

"Come on," I said, rising to my feet. "We should get you back to your hotel. You're going to pass out on me."

"All right," he said with another yawn. He stood and closed out the tab, dropping some cash on the table. "Let's go."

We took the elevator to the lobby.

"Where are you staying?"

"Here," I told him.

"Oh. Well, fuck. I'll take the Subway back by myself."

"Okay."

He reached out for me, taking my hand in his. Such a familiar feeling. All the years apart falling away. "Unless … you want to come with me."

Our eyes met, and I saw the real question there. If I went with him, I'd stay the night. We'd definitely hook up. And I *did* want that, but it would be a mistake.

"You and I both know what will happen if I come to your hotel with you."

He circled my empty ring finger. "You're divorced ..."

"I am. And you? We haven't talked about it all night. I assumed for a reason."

He winced. "I mean ... we're on a break."

I pulled back gently. "A break isn't broken up. I taught you that."

"Fuck." He stepped away from me and ran his hands back through his hair. "Why can't I get enough of you, Josie? Why does it feel like torture every time we do this?"

"I don't know," I whispered. "I wish I knew."

His hands went into my hair, and he pulled my face to his, pressing a firm kiss to my lips. We both could give in then, sink into that kiss and forget the rest of the world. My head was spinning from the taste of his lips. It would be so easy to drag him upstairs. We'd regret it in the morning, but it would be worth it for one more night.

But I withdrew. Because whoever the girl was that he was on a break with didn't deserve this. Even if I loved him—and I would *always* love him—I wanted more than this, and we couldn't have it.

"Good night, Maddox."

He sighed and dropped his forehead to mine. "Good night, Josie."

Then, he released me in a rush and hurried out of the lobby of the hotel. I watched his retreating back until it was out of sight. My night of celebration bringing with it another broken heart.

26

SCAD

OCTOBER 28, 2016

"Holy shit, look at you!" Marley gasped.

I flung my arms around my best friend, heedless of everyone's eyes on me. We were at the SCAD Film Festival, attending a cocktail party dedicated to the honored graduates of the university. It was at this very festival where I'd failed horribly as a director and gotten my big break, all in the same night. I also couldn't think of the festival without thinking about Maddox, who Marley had come with to the party.

Because of course we were being honored in the same year. Of course we were.

"I missed you so much," I told Marley.

"I missed you too." She pulled back and assessed me. "I love this dress on you."

"Thank you. Amelia designed it."

Marley nodded, her jaw set. "She's really talented."

It was as close as I would get to bringing up Derek in front of her. Not that she was rushing to drag Maddox over to see me. He was across the room, against a wall, avoiding talking to as many people as possible. I'd seen him as soon as he and Mars entered. She'd hurried away to greet him. A pinball between the two of us.

A throat cleared next to me. The real reason Mars was pinballing. "Are you going to introduce me, darling?"

I withdrew from Marley and gestured to Craig Van der Berg. "Marley, this is my fiancé, Craig. Craig, this is Marley. She's going to be a bridesmaid."

"Damn right I am!" she said cheerfully. She held her hand out, and Craig shook it.

"Pleasure to meet you. Any friend of Josie's is a friend of mine."

I'd known Craig for years. In fact, his father, Henrick, was the one who had given me the big break. Craig came and went from the studio where I played Cassie Herrington. But it was only in the last year that we'd really gotten to know each other.

We'd hit it off, and I'd let him pull me into his orbit like a runaway train. Craig was rich, *rich* in a way that I hardly even comprehended. And it wasn't like I had grown up poor or didn't have millions from my years on *Academy*. But he treated wealth like something else entirely. And he had drawn me in like a moth to a flame.

Not that I'd fallen for him because of his money. Far from it. I'd been uncomfortable with the displays at first until I got to know the man underneath the wealth. He was charming, sweet, considerate. He wasn't a Southern gentleman, pulling out chairs and opening doors, but he had this aura about him that made people do things for him. So, I was always taken care of.

Marley and Craig talked animatedly for a while

before she went back across the room to Maddox. My eyes followed her, and I frowned when I realized there was someone else with him. And I recognized her from his profile online—Teena.

I found it hard to believe that they were dating almost four years later ... and he hadn't proposed. I'd hidden his profile, but still, I was sure that Mars would have mentioned it.

Maddox looked up then, and our eyes connected across the ballroom. His girlfriend next to him. My fiancé next to me. And still, we were the only two people in the room.

"Honey?" Craig said, breaking my concentration.

I dropped Maddox's gaze and turned away. "Hmm? Sorry."

"My father wants to introduce us to some friends of his."

"Oh, of course," I said.

I promised to put Maddox Nelson out of my mind and enjoy the rest of the night. Just because we had history didn't mean it had to ruin my night. I was here with my wonderful fiancé, and that was what mattered.

I'd gotten an honorary plaque that the festival promised to mail to me, and now, the night felt over. But everyone wanted more of my time, and drinks were still flowing. Craig had disappeared to have cigars with some friends. I was currently regretting drinking one too many drinks and wondering if I could get out of this conversation, find him, and leave. But I didn't even know where he had gone off to.

"Hey," Marley said, sliding in next to me. "I'm going to head out."

"Already?"

"It's late," she reminded me.

"Can I come with you?" I joked.

She giggled. "And disappoint your many adoring fans?"

"Nah, these people all think I'm beneath them because I sold out and went mainstream."

Marley nearly choked. "That's ridiculous."

"Showbiz."

"Well, I think you're fabulous."

"Thanks. I'll miss you. Hang out again soon?"

"Anytime." Marley squeezed my hand. "You should talk to him."

I blinked at her. "Who?"

She gave me a knowing look. "Josie."

"Oh," I whispered, glancing down at my empty drink. "Maddox, you mean."

"What do I know? I've only had one relationship, and it was a mess. But he's my brother, and you're always going to be in each other's world."

"I know we are."

"And I hate this back-and-forth."

I laughed. "Do it for you, you mean?"

"Would you?" she asked with a grin.

"Fine. Yes. I'll be cordial. I don't know where the fuck Craig went anyway."

"Thank you. He headed that way," Marley said,

pointing to an adjoining room. "Let me know how it goes."

I nodded and watched her walk away. I wished that I could do the same. As much as I wanted to see Maddox, everything about it was complicated. Especially since his girlfriend and my fiancé were both here. Craig hadn't noticed that Maddox and I had been sneaking glances at each other all night, avoiding each other's orbit. I didn't know if his girlfriend had either. For his sake, I hoped not.

With a deep breath, I made my excuses to everyone around me and headed toward the other room. As I reached the entrance, I could hear raised voices on the other side.

"She's engaged again, and you're still waiting for her to come back!" a woman practically yelled.

"That is not ..." Maddox's voice was unmistakable.

My feet stilled just before the entrance to the room. Were they talking about ... me?

"It is!" she yelled. "You've been tracking her all fucking night, Maddox. I know you well enough for that. We've been together almost four years."

"I don't know what you want me to say, Teena. I'm here with you."

She laughed, and it was a train running off the tracks. "And I'm the idiot who's been waiting for you to see that I'm right in front of you."

Before I could move away quick enough, Teena came crashing in through the door, nearly hurtling into me. She reminded me so much of the girl that Maddox had dated in college. Blonde and mousy and nondescript in almost every way. Her eyes were red and puffy with tears in her lashes. She took one look at me, and a sob escaped her mouth.

"He's all yours," she gasped and then hurried away.

I was momentarily frozen in shock. Teena had just blamed me for a breakup that I had had no part in. But then ... hadn't I? I hadn't stayed away from Maddox over the years, and he hadn't stayed away from me either.

Then, Maddox was there. He saw me standing there, and something shifted in him. His eyes went hard and flat. "You," he growled.

I shivered at that one word from him. I'd never heard him speak like that to me. I held my hands up in surrender. "I came by to say hi."

"Why?" he snapped.

"Marley actually ... she thought we should ... reconcile."

It sounded stupid now. Standing here, I could see that there was no reconciliation on his face. That this could never go back to how it had been. Not after what Teena had thrown at him. Not after I'd married Martin. Not after any of it really.

"Why are you always there at the worst time? Why can't you let me be?"

"Don't blame this on me," I said, my own anger coming to the surface. "You were the one shooting me looks all night."

"I was trying to avoid you!"

"Maybe you should have acted like it didn't matter. Because ... it clearly did."

"Of course it fucking mattered, Josie. You ... you are

231

always here. You're always around. You're embedded in my skin." He shook his head and stepped away. "And I want you gone."

My heart panged at that. Still, I steeled myself. We needed to have this conversation. Good or bad.

So, I followed him into the next room.

"Well, I don't think that's going to change anytime soon, do you? Marley sent me here because we'll *always* be together, Maddox. We've known each other our entire lives. We're not suddenly going to stop seeing each other. We need to find a way to live with this."

"Fuck that," he spat.

I balked. "What?"

"I don't want to *live like this*," he snarled. "I don't want to live with you, and somehow, I can't fucking live without you. I hate it. I hate all of it. I hate fucking seeing you with someone else."

"You came with someone else too!"

Maddox scoffed. "It's hardly comparable."

"Why? Because you were with Teena for four years and never popped the question?"

"Oh, it's so much better to know someone for six months and get engaged? That worked so well for you last time."

"When you know, you know."

He laughed. "Right. And you think Craig Van der Berg is *the one*?"

My hackles rose at the way he'd said that. "So what if I do?"

"You're not serious," he said with a shake of his head.

He paced away from me. I'd never seen him boil over

before. He was always so restrained. It had to be the combination of the breakup and me being here with Craig that had sent him over the edge.

"You see what you're doing, right?" he asked, facing me again. "He's the son of the owner of the company. The son of the guy who got you your break."

"So?"

Maddox's face hardened. "What's that line? You can't honestly tell me you're not marrying him for his money. Oh, wait. Or are you marrying him for his father's money?"

I narrowed my eyes. I recognized the reference to the famous lines from one of my favorite movies—*Gentlemen Prefer Blondes* with Marilyn Monroe. I didn't know how many times we'd watched it together.

"Don't fucking quote that at me."

"Why not? It's true!"

"I am not marrying Craig for money!"

"What else does she say? 'A man being rich is like a girl being pretty.' It's a classic Marilyn move."

"Is that what you really think of me?" I asked, dangerously low.

"I never would have before. When you married Martin, I thought you were a fool for love. But now? Fuck, Jos. What even are you doing?"

I clenched my hands into fists. "You're out of line. You're mad and taking it out on me. I am not to blame for your breakup with Teena."

"Oh no, of course not. It's *never* your fault. Nothing is ever your fault."

"You don't have to disparage my relationship because

233

yours ended," I snapped back. "And I don't deserve this. I'm not going to stand around and let you be an asshole to me."

Maddox shook his head. "Fine. Then, just leave."

"I am!" I shouted, turning toward the exit.

My anger felt like a roiling snake under my skin. I saw red at his unjust accusations. I was so furious that I was shaking as I crossed into the other room.

But as soon as I was out on the Savannah streets, I slumped against a door and felt myself deflate. I hadn't wanted to get into that fight with Maddox. And now, things were a fucking mess between us. I didn't even know if I could fix this after that.

I dialed Marley's number, but it went straight to voicemail. She must already be asleep. I should find Craig, but instead, I headed out onto the streets and walked off the gnawing feeling that Maddox and I had made a huge mistake.

Eight months later, Craig and I were married on the beach in Santa Monica. Lila and Marley were bridesmaids. It was a beautiful summer wedding.

But that gnawing feeling never left. And we were divorced the following February due to irreconcilable differences.

In the back of my mind, I wondered if I had been swept up in his extravagant lifestyle, his easy, excessive ways, his money.

If Maddox was right all along.

27

SAVANNAH
PRESENT

"And that's a wrap!" Jimmy announced to the cast and crew.

We all applauded as the last six weeks of filming came to a close. It was hard to believe that it had all gone so fast. And that I had nothing else lined up after it.

"Congrats, darling," Martin said dramatically. He pulled me into a hug. "You were as brilliant as ever."

"Thanks, Marty."

I went around the room, hugging everyone. Iris had tears in her eyes as she hugged me tight. It was surreal to think that this was the actual finale for this show that we'd dedicated a decade. She pressed a kiss to my cheek and released me with a smile.

Then, my eyes found the person I was looking for, and I skipped over to Maddox, throwing my arms around him. "Wrap day!"

He laughed and pressed a firm kiss to my lips. The last couple weeks had been the best of our long-storied time together. In those intervening years when we had avoided each other and yearned and pined and fought, I never would have thought that we could end up here. That after the words we'd spoken to each other in hate, we'd be able to live so harmoniously in love. It was as if this was how it was always supposed to be, and we'd taken the circuitous route to get here.

"So proud of you," he said.

"Aww, thanks. I can't believe it's over."

"I still have a few weeks of post-production."

"Well, done for me at least."

"The easy part is over," he joked.

"Hey!" I swatted at him, but he ducked and drew me in for another kiss.

"Now, we can have a long night in."

I smirked at him. "As lovely as that sounds, you're forgetting one thing."

His face was blank.

"Wrap party."

He groaned. "Must we?"

"We must. Amelia designed me a new dress for the occasion. She and Ash will be there."

"Together?" He arched an eyebrow.

"Who knows with them? They're like sharks circling."

"Fine. I'll go for you."

I winked at him. "Much obliged."

When Maddox picked me up a few hours later, his jaw nearly dropped to the ground at the sight of me. The dress Amelia had made for me was a revelation.

Seafoam-green silk that hugged all my features with a slit to mid-thigh, a slouchy front that showed off ample cleavage, and an open, lace-up back. I twirled for him in my strappy heeled sandals.

"Jesus Christ." His hand slid down the silk from my waist to my hip. "You look stunning. Are you sure we have to go to the party?"

"And not show off my dress?"

He leaned in close. "It'll look better on my floor."

"I like this side of you," I teased, grabbing his shirt and tugging him against me.

Our lips met, and a voice cleared behind us.

I pulled away to find my mom standing in the living room. "Don't you look lovely?"

"Thanks," I said.

"Where are you off to?" she asked.

"Wrap party."

"You finished the movie today?"

Was it just me, or did she look disappointed? I hadn't seen much of her in the last couple of weeks. Despite asking me to stay, she had made herself scarce. Always off with her new beau. It didn't help that we'd had long days on set and I spent the weekends with Maddox. Maybe I'd been as scarce as she had.

"We did."

"When are you going back to LA?" she asked softly.

"Oh. I haven't decided yet. I'm in no hurry. I'm still waiting to hear about an audition. It would film in Atlanta though, I think."

"Okay. Well, maybe we can have dinner before you go. Just the two of us."

I swallowed and nodded. "I'd like that."

"It sounds like a great idea," Maddox agreed.

"Are you spending the evening with Roger?"

I realized that I hadn't seen him around the house in at least a week. Had it been longer? Maybe he was away on business. He didn't live in town as far as I knew.

"No, I'm not."

"Is everything all right?"

"We ... broke up," my mother said with a small shrug, as if it didn't bother her but I knew it did.

"What? Why? He seemed besotted."

"Ah well, unfortunately, my reputation precedes me."

My jaw dropped. "He left you because he heard the rumors about Edward?"

My mother nodded once. "It's fine. It's happened before. No real loss as far as I'm concerned." She said the words, but they held no feeling. And for the first time, I really saw the consequence of my mother's bad reputation. It wasn't just tittering women, shunning her on the streets. It was also that she couldn't move on from what had happened because no man would touch her when they found out.

"We're going to the Talmadge Center for the wrap party if you want to join us," I found myself offering before I could help it.

Maddox shot me a look of surprise and maybe ... pride?

"Oh, no. You two have fun. Don't worry about me." She stepped forward and took my hand. "I'm glad to see you happy."

I didn't know what came over me. I'd been mad at my

mom for so long. But things were so good with Maddox that I didn't have it in me to be mad at anyone right now. I put my arms around her and held her tight. She startled. We hadn't hugged since I had been a kid. But slowly, her arms came around me.

"See you later, Mom," I said as I pulled back.

A smile lit her beautiful features. "Good night, Josie."

Maddox took my arm, and we headed out of my mom's house. I felt light as a feather. I never thought that six weeks would fix what was broken between me and my mom. And maybe it wasn't fixed, but it was at least mending. That was more than I'd believed possible.

Maddox opened my door to his Jeep. His eyes soft. His smile adoring. He said everything in that one look that we didn't even need to speak about what had just happened. I loved that he knew me well enough to know how much this meant to me.

He parked downtown, and we walked into the Talmadge Center, a ballroom that hosted events. The party was on the rooftop bar, overlooking the Savannah River. Lots of weddings happened in this venue. Amelia had confessed that Ash had offered the space to the studio for the wrap party. I was surprised by his generosity, especially considering our general animosity. Perhaps I thought the worst of Ash Talmadge, but he was just as varied as my mother. I wasn't sure I liked having to think of everyone as nuanced people.

"Josie!" Amelia said when we entered.

The bar was already packed with cast and crew for the movie. I could hardly believe how many unfamiliar faces there were though. Lots of local people must have been invited as well.

"Hey you," I said.

"Ash reserved a table for us. You can sit with us. I want you to meet my cousin."

I glanced at Maddox, and he shrugged. "A table with Ash Talmadge."

Amelia laughed. "I swear he's not as bad as y'all make him out to be. Whatever Ash you knew before isn't who he is. I wish you'd all get along."

"I want what's best for you, Mia. I've just known him a long, *long* time."

"I've known him my entire life," she said, taking my arm. "Forget the past for tonight."

"All right. I'll do my best."

"Okay, good." She dragged me across the room. "Josie, this is my cousin, Marina Hartage. Marina, this is Josephine Reynolds."

Marina Hartage was homecoming-queen beautiful. She looked like the kind of girl who was as comfortable digging in the dirt as winning a beauty pageant. She had almost-cartoon-wide blue eyes and a heart-shaped face with pouty, large lips. Her shoulder-length brown hair was parted down the middle and straight as a pin with '90s Rachel bangs. And it worked for her.

"Nice to meet you."

She shook my hand. "I've heard so much about you. I used to watch *Academy* when I was growing up. Crazy to actually meet you."

"Were you obsessed with Martin too?"

"I was until the divorce." Marina shrugged. "Broke my heart to see that."

"Same," I admitted. "What are you in town for?"

"Next week, we're all sailing the Intracoastal Waterway up to Charleston. I decided to fly down and do the big trek with Amelia, Derek, and Ash."

"Marina runs Hartage Boating with her brother, Daron," Amelia explained. "It's a successful boating and tour company in Charleston."

"Yeah, Dare is running the business while I'm gone. He's pretty pissed about it," she said with a laugh. "But he got to do it last time."

"I'd heard y'all were doing that. Not my speed, but I bet y'all will have the best time."

Ash arched an eyebrow at me. "What? You don't want to live on a sailboat with us for three days?"

"Ash Talmadge, you have known me for more than two decades. Would you *ever* think I'd want to get on a sailboat?"

He smirked. "Fair."

"Did someone say Ash Talmadge?" a voice boomed from behind us.

Ash turned around, confusion on his face, and then he broke out into a genial laugh. "Nolan!"

He clapped hands with a guy that I'd never seen before, but dear God, he was attractive. Taller even than Ash in a sharp navy-blue suit. He had dark brown hair with eyes the color of the sea in a thunderstorm and a strong square jaw. Dimples appeared in his cheeks when he shook hands with Ash.

"Fuck, man, what are you doing here?"

"Holden Holdings was part of the team to help with the movie. The director sent us an invitation to the party, and since I was already in town on business, I thought I'd swing by. Didn't think you'd be here."

"It's my building," Ash said with a laugh.

"Should have known."

Amelia softly cleared her throat. "Introductions perhaps?"

Ash's eyes found hers, and the light in them was so bright. "Right. Yeah, sure. This is Nolan Holden. We went to Duke together. His family runs Holden Holdings, originally based out of Williamsburg."

"Yes, we're now headquartered in Charleston," Nolan filled in.

"I heard that your father is stepping down and naming you CEO."

"That's right. Rob is coming home for it too."

"You're going to get him out of New York?"

"And back where he belongs," Nolan said. His eyes found me, and he smiled. "Sorry to interrupt your evening. You're Josephine Reynolds."

"That's me," I said with a smile.

"Talent and beauty, all in one package."

I laughed, and Maddox put an arm around my waist, claiming me. I kind of loved it.

But it was Marina who made a gagging noise. I hadn't noticed, but she'd essentially slid behind Amelia so that she was invisible to Nolan Holden. But at that one sound, his face snapped to her, and something predatory was there for a beat before disappearing.

"Marina," he said, drawing out her name. Low and tempting.

"Nolan," she practically growled.

"What a surprise."

Marina narrowed her eyes at him. Heat bristled in the short distance between them. "I'm sure it is."

Amelia gave her a questioning look, but Marina just shook her head.

"It's been a while. Miss me?"

Marina glared daggers at him. "That isn't the word I'd use."

Nolan just smiled wider.

But Marina looked like a rabbit ready to flee a fox. "If you'll excuse me."

"Marina, wait," Amelia said, hurrying after her.

"What was that about?" I asked.

Nolan shrugged his powerful shoulders, feigning innocence. "I have no idea."

We were interrupted from asking more by someone mistakenly handing Jimmy a microphone. "Can I get Martin and Josephine up here?"

I rolled my eyes. "Lord, preserve me."

Maddox snickered. "Have fun."

Marty found me just as we reached the front of the room. He took my hand and held it aloft. "Wrap party!"

I laughed and effortlessly extracted my hand from his.

"Thank you all so much for coming out tonight. We'd love to celebrate all of you with an open bar!" Jimmy cried. The crowd cheered. "We wouldn't be here tonight without every one of you. You have made this movie what it is. I'm so happy to have Martin and Josephine back for this movie, and I can't wait for it to be in theaters."

Jimmy droned on, thanking all the individual units who were part of the movie. He toasted me and Martin a few times. It felt ridiculous, but I was too giddy not to indulge. Maddox held his glass aloft to me from his seat at Ash's reserved table. Where he'd likely stay all night, letting me be the belle of the ball, as I was prone to do. But this time, he wasn't mad that I was in my element while he was on the outskirts. We were precisely where we needed to be. This was who we were, and we might be different, but that was our strength, not our weakness.

When Jimmy finally finished speaking, I crept off the stage. As I had done earlier, I went around the room, saying my thank-yous until even I was tired from the exertion. I found Amelia alone with her back to the party, her elbows against the brick railing, looking out across the river.

"Are you trying to escape too?"

Amelia laughed. "Nah, Ash went to get drinks. And I'm mostly sad that Marina left."

"What happened with her and Nolan?"

She shrugged. "She wouldn't even tell me. Said she needed some space. Hopefully, she'll confess to me while we're on the boat this week."

"He probably fucked her and fucked her over."

"You'd think, but Marina doesn't get upset about that kind of thing. It had to be personal."

"Well, I hope she tells you what happened."

"Same." Amelia sighed and hung her head. "Can I talk to you about something else too?"

"Oh boy," I muttered.

"You can probably guess, but, uh, Lila?"

"Yeah," I said hesitantly.

"I don't talk about her or ask about her, but Derek called to discuss the trip, and he ..."

"Yeah?"

"Ash doesn't know?"

"No."

"And you agreed to tell him after we get back?"

"Derek said he would," I confirmed.

"I wish he'd never told me. I feel real sick about knowing and not telling Ash. I don't even know Lila. She was two years ahead of me at St. Catherine's. We didn't really interact. But how do you think he'll react when he finds out?" Amelia asked softly.

"That ... I don't know."

"Do you think he'll ... try to stop the wedding?"

I put my hand on Amelia's. "You're only hurting yourself, asking yourself these what-ifs."

"I know, but fuck, the bad timing. Did Cole really have to propose to Lila right now?"

A glass shattered behind us.

We both whirled around. Ash Talmadge stood before us. A drink had slipped out of his hand. The liquid was on the bottom of his suit pants and glass all over the floor. His face was pale, and his eyes were dark when they locked on Amelia.

"What?" he asked, hard and flat.

"Ash," Amelia gasped. Her hand went to her mouth in horror at what she'd unknowingly just done.

"Cole ... proposed to Lila."

"Yes," I said. I wanted to step in front of Amelia. I could weather his anger. Amelia didn't deserve it. She had been the one there for him all these years while he was dealing with his shit.

"You knew?" he said, still looking at Amelia.

"Yes, but ..."

"Did Derek know?"

Amelia opened and closed her mouth. "He ..."

"Of course he did. Of course he fucking did."

"Ash ..."

"Everyone knew," he finished.

Amelia took a step forward, reaching to touch his sleeve. But Ash flinched and jerked backward. I'd never gotten along with Ash, but even I felt bad for him in that moment. And just as bad for Amelia, who looked ready to cry by that one act of rejection.

"Hey, what's going on over here?" Maddox asked, striding toward us.

Ash shook his head. "I'm ... going to go."

Maddox watched him walk away in confusion. "What just happened?"

"He found out about Lila," I said.

"Fuck," Maddox said.

"I should go after him," Amelia choked out.

"No," Maddox and I said together. That would not go well.

Maddox sighed. "I'll do it. Let me make sure he gets in a car home and doesn't do anything stupid."

"Thank you," I told him as I put a protective arm around Amelia.

"I didn't mean for that to happen."

"Hey, it's going to be okay. He needs to process."

"I shouldn't have hidden it from him."

"Maybe not," I admitted. "But we all agreed to. That's not on you."

"Fuck. Fuck everything. Fuck this timing. I just thought we were ..." She trailed off and swiped under her eyes. "I guess it doesn't matter. I'm ... going to get someone to clean this up."

"Are you sure?"

"Yeah," she said and then went in search of help.

I sank into a seat. What a night. I should probably tell Cole, Derek, and Mars what had gone down. No one was going to like that it had happened this way. But it was done now. No more hiding.

I pulled out my phone to shoot them a text and saw that I had a missed call from an unknown number. They'd left a voicemail. I brought the phone to my ear and tried to drown out the party to listen.

"Hey, Josephine. It's with deep regret that I make this call. We greatly enjoyed your audition for the part of Beatrice, but unfortunately, we've had to go in a different direction. Thank you so much for your audition, and we hope to see you again soon."

The voicemail ended, and I was frozen in place.

The color drained out of my face as fast as the bottom drained out of my career.

I hadn't gotten the job.

I hadn't gotten the job.

28

SAVANNAH
PRESENT

"Well, I got Ash into a cab," Maddox said when he found me downstairs in the lobby. "How's Amelia doing?"

"It's over, Maddox."

He paused. A flash of fear flashing on his face. He asked very gently, "What is over?"

"My career."

The fear disappeared, and in its place was confusion. This wasn't where he'd thought the conversation was going. I hadn't been honest about what my life had been like in the intervening years since *Academy* had ended. I avoided talking about it at all. Just focused on this one last audition. The one that I had been sure I had in the bag.

It had been the best audition of my life. Better even than *Academy*.

I was starting to think that I'd only gotten that job because I already *was* Cassie Herrington. Henrick Van der Berg had wanted someone just like *me* to play his heroine. He'd plucked me out of obscurity to do it. In my darkest days with Craig, he'd told me that I couldn't act and had only gotten the job because I didn't *have* to act. I'd screamed at him for saying it. I'd hated him then, so I'd ignored his hurtful comments. Millions of followers, eight seasons of the show, and one movie later, and I was clearly a good actor. Wasn't I?

"Why would you say that?"

"I didn't get the role," I said, dropping my head into my hands. "They called and left a message. They said they were going in a different direction."

"Oh, Josie, I'm so sorry. I know you were really looking forward to that part."

"I was," I whispered.

"But there will be other auditions and other jobs. I'm sure—"

"No," I cut him off as I looked up at him.

He frowned. "No?"

I shook my head so hard that my hair flew in a fan. "No. There are no other parts. No other jobs or auditions. There's nothing left, Maddox."

"Josie, I'm sure there are other roles for you."

"There are no other fish in the sea. This was the last one."

"I can see how you would feel that way but—"

"It's not..." I said, my voice going high. I tried to hold back the tears. I didn't want to cry. But tears were my calling card. The one thing that had always come easy to me. "I don't know how to say this."

"Hey," Maddox said, getting down on my level and taking my hands. "You can tell me anything."

I looked up into those sincere, dark eyes and knew he really believed that.

"I've been auditioning constantly since *Academy* ended, Maddox. *Constantly*. And I've gotten hundreds of rejections. My agent keeps telling me the same thing that you did. That there's something out there for me. *Academy* was too successful for me not to step into other roles. Martin has. So, why wouldn't I, right?" I swiped at the tear on my cheek. "But men are allowed to age in Hollywood, and somehow, at not even thirty-two, I'm too old for the roles that people want to give me. I'm too old to play a high school student. I'm too young to play serious roles. Trust me, I've heard it all. There are *no* acting jobs for me out there. I'm just Cassie Herrington."

"They're all fucking stupid then. I watched you work for the last six weeks. Sure, maybe you were Cassie Herrington, but that's not who you are. You put everything into that role. They're all idiots for not wanting you."

"That doesn't change the facts," I yelled, feeling the anger and resentment that I'd held toward myself bubbling to the surface. "It doesn't change the fact that I have no career. I have this movie, and then it's over."

"It's not over."

"It is! How can you be so calm?! It's over."

I pushed away from him and stormed toward the entrance. He jogged after me, catching me around the middle and holding me close to him.

"Josie, it's going to be okay."

I pulled out of his embrace. The tears were coming harder, and I just wanted to collapse. "Nothing is okay. I don't even know how you can look at me. Why would you want someone like me? All I've done is hurt you."

"We hurt each other. I was as much in the wrong in the past as you were. I said things I regret, and I won't be that person again," he said, reaching for me again. "I'm not going to fight with you. I'm going to fight *for* you."

A sob escaped me at those words. "Maddox."

He pulled me in, and the tears ran into his shoulder. "Hey, I'm here. You can be mad at your career. You can be mad at the industry. You can be mad at Martin. I'll allow that too."

I hiccuped on a laugh. "I bet."

He kissed my hair. "But you're not mad at me. I wish you'd told me, so we could have dealt with this together."

"I was embarrassed," I admitted. "You're so successful. You have your own studio. Your own company. And I ... I have *Academy*."

"*Academy* was what you *wanted* though," he reminded me. "You went after it with full vigor."

"And now, anything I go after, I don't get."

"Then flip the script."

I arched an eyebrow at him. "What do you mean?"

"Don't do what everyone thinks you're going to do. Stop doing what they expect. Give up on the idea that following the Hollywood mold is what you need. You didn't get into acting by following their advice. You met a stranger in an alley and started your entire career."

"Yeah, but who is going to give me a second break like that?"

"*You* are," he said, taking my shoulders in his hands.

"You're in the unique position where you can do whatever you want."

"I want to act."

"Then act. Maybe audition for smaller roles, do voice acting, work in the theater, try Broadway. I don't know, Josie, but you're capable. Personally, I think you should direct your own film. It's what you always wanted to do. You pivoted because acting was more viable. Now, it's time to follow your heart."

I choked out a laugh. "My directing debut was a huge bust."

"And now, you have a decade of experience on a television set. I bet you can use that to your advantage to make something new and interesting. Something you love. And why *not*? You know people in the industry who will work with you. I have a studio here in town that you can use."

"I could ... use your studio?" I asked, momentarily lost in shock. His studio was a multimillion-dollar complex, and there was no fucking way I'd be able to afford it. It was basically being used for only the highest-dollar projects. I still couldn't believe we'd gotten it for *Academy*.

"Sure. Why not?"

"Um ... I could never afford it."

Maddox shot me a look. "I invented it. And there are three people in the entire world who can run it. I trained the other two people, so I wouldn't have to be there every day. *That's* why it costs studios so much to work with me. I'm not charging you."

I opened my mouth and then realized I had nothing

to say. What he was offering was outrageous and so utterly generous.

"I ... I don't even have an idea."

He shrugged. "So what? If you're not auditioning, you'll figure out what you want to work on. You have money. You have time. The project will come to you. I believe in you."

Could I do what he was suggesting? Was that even possible? My agent would probably have a fit if I told her that I didn't want any more auditions. But it wasn't her career; it was mine. I had Maddox. He was here, fighting for me to be the best version of myself. I'd never thought I'd have that. I'd never thought any of this could be possible.

"What do you think? Tell me what's going on in that beautiful head of yours."

"I'm lucky to have you."

He beamed. "Well, that's true."

I stood on my tiptoes and pressed a kiss to his lips. He wrapped his arms tight around my waist and deepened the kiss.

"Thank you," I whispered. I sniffled again.

"For the kiss?"

I rolled my eyes at him. "For talking me down. For ... believing in me."

"Josie," he said, cupping my cheek, "I love you."

Tears came to my eyes all over again at those words. "I love you too."

"God, you don't know how good it is to hear you say that."

"Oh, I think I do."

He dropped his mouth on mine again. It was slow and possessive. With those three words, I belonged to him. I always had, but we'd sealed it. There was nowhere else I wanted to be. Nowhere else that I felt safe and cared for. Maddox was willing to fight for me. He'd loved me when I was nobody and when I was a television star and when I was once again a nobody. He loved me just how I was. And somewhere in all of my own panic about my career, I'd forgotten how valuable that was. I didn't have to do all of this alone.

"Come on," he said, taking my hand and drawing me out of the building.

"Where are we going?"

"Home."

Twenty minutes later, Maddox was opening the door to Gran's house. He let Walt outside, got him inside with a bone, and then tugged me into the renovated master bedroom.

"I love you," he said.

He kissed my shoulder.

"I love you."

He dragged down the zipper on my dress.

"I love you."

Another kiss at the base of my neck.

"I love you."

My dress puddled on the ground.

"Oh, look. I was right. I do like it better on the ground."

I laughed and reached for him, stripping him out of his button-up and slacks. We fell onto the bed. Our bodies intertwined among the sheets. His hands traced a map of my skin. Mine moved through his dark hair, running through the curly strands. Our lips molded together. We writhed against each other. No distance or time between us. Every touch and kiss and feel heated and intense.

As if sparks were under my skin, and they ignited every place he touched.

I couldn't get enough of him. Couldn't get close enough. Our chests and hips pushed together. Our legs tangled. Our arms locked around each other. And still, I wanted more. I wanted to feel all of him until we were one.

"Please," I gasped against his lips.

"I love you," he said again as he kissed along my jaw.

"More," I pleaded.

The scruff of his five o'clock shadow dragged along my neck as he brought his kisses lower and then across my collarbone.

"I want all of you, Josie."

"I'm yours."

He lifted my leg higher around his hip, angling our bodies to meet. The first touch of him at my entrance had me seeing stars. I was so enraptured with him that everything was heightened tenfold.

"Is this what you want?" he asked, his voice low and throaty.

"Yes. Oh God, yes."

"Tell me you love me."

"I love you so much," I said, claiming his mouth again.

He thrust inside of me in the same moment, and we

both cried out at the joining. We fit together like the missing puzzle piece. Whole and complete.

We could barely move in this position, but we didn't need to. Just the rocking of our hips was enough friction to push me toward the edge. With all the heat and contact, it was as emotional as it was physical. A coupling born of love and not just primal need. But I wanted him here in my heart as much as I wanted him here inside of me.

"Fuck," he grunted against my shoulder. "Fuck, you feel so good, Josie."

"Yes. I'm so close. Come with me, Maddox."

And then, somehow, we got even closer. Our bodies pressed so tight together that when I hit my climax, he could feel it shudder through me.

"Josie," he groaned, and then he came with me.

Neither of us was able to hold back from the other. Everything completely bare. And I'd never been happier.

I'd shredded myself down to the core. Accepted that I might have no career anymore. That I might have to take some inexplicable new venture to continue working. And when that had happened, Maddox had been there to catch me when I fell. And all I'd done was fall harder for him.

29

SAVANNAH

PRESENT

The next morning, I was still wrapped in Maddox's arms, and I never wanted to move again.

He kissed my shoulder as I stirred. "Morning."

"Mmm," I said, rolling toward him. "Good morning."

"I could get used to waking up like this."

"That so?"

"Oh, yes." He flipped me over and settled himself between my legs as he focused on my breasts.

"Oh," I gasped when he sucked a nipple into his mouth.

"I wonder how you taste this morning."

"I haven't even brushed my teeth."

He laughed. "I wasn't planning to kiss those lips."

Then, he scooted down and settled his head between my thighs until I screamed into the morning. He gave me a satisfied smirk, and we ended up kissing anyway as he buried himself inside of me. The night had been languid and all-consuming. The morning was fast and desperate as I clawed at his back. We came together just as hard as before, leaving me panting on the sheets.

"I need a shower," he said when he collapsed next to me.

"Seconded."

"Together?" He ran a hand over my hip bone.

"If we shower together, we're not going to get clean."

He gave me a devious look. "I like this even more."

I laughed and kissed him again. "Just let me brush my teeth, and you can have the shower. I'll shower after breakfast."

"Where do you want to go?"

"I'll see what you have in the fridge."

He grimaced. "Probably not much, honestly."

"I'll make it work." I kissed his nose and then hopped out of the bed.

After cleaning myself up, I headed into the kitchen. Maddox had let Walt out, and he now had his head in a bowl of food. "Good boy," I said, scratching his head.

I pulled open the fridge and realized he was right. There really wasn't much in there. He'd been living at the studio and eating out all the time. Then, my eyes drifted to the box of Gran's recipes.

A smirk hit my features as I reached for it and dug out the biscuits and gravy recipe that Maddox loved so much.

When he surfaced from the shower, the biscuits were just coming out of the oven, soft and fluffy. They even *looked* like Gran's biscuits. I stirred the gravy I'd made from scratch. I'd felt lucky that Maddox had sausage in the freezer. Everything smelled incredible.

Maddox's hair was still wet when he stepped into the

kitchen with wide eyes. "It smells like home in here. I thought I didn't have anything in the house."

"You had flour, butter, and sugar. I can make pretty much anything with that," I said with a wink.

He reached out to touch a biscuit, and I smacked his hand.

"Hey!"

"They're too hot."

"They look just like ... Gran's," he said in awe.

"I'm a pretty good cook. I thought I'd give it a shot. I know how much you loved her cooking."

"Marry me," he said.

"Don't get ahead of yourself," I said as I dished up breakfast. "You haven't even tried it yet."

I set the food down on the dining room table. We'd sat here with Gran and Gramps so many times over the years. It felt surreal that we were here together now without them, re-creating Gran's recipes.

Maddox practically shoveled the food into his mouth. "How ... how did you do this?"

"Made with love."

"I stand by my earlier statement. Marry me."

I shook my head and reached for his hand. "I love you."

"Okay. Fine. We'll wait. Move in then."

"Because I can cook?"

"Because I'm crazy about you, Josie. I want you here all the time. I want you to move in. I want you to have half of the closet. I want your stuff to mingle with mine. I want you to use the kitchen and, yeah, try out all of Gran's old recipes. I want to share this life with you. So, move in with me."

With my heart full to bursting, I nodded. "Yes. Okay. I'll move in."

He kissed me hard and then stood with his plate. "I need seconds."

I cracked up. I had a feeling I'd be making this for him forever. And I loved that idea.

I moved in the next day. Mom was glad that I'd agreed to stay in Savannah for the time being even if it wasn't in her house. We'd agreed to meet for dinner regularly since I was less busy. Dad seemed unsurprised that I'd decided to stay. He'd known I was in love with Maddox again before I did, apparently. And he wholeheartedly approved. He just requested that we come back to Atlanta and see him again soon. Which really meant, we needed to stay longer, so he and Maddox could draw together, but I wasn't complaining.

Now that I had time to myself again, I'd taken to sitting in Gran's rocking chair on the back porch, reading my mother's journal. Maddox still had post-production work to do. So, he was busy most days. I didn't have anything official to do until we went on a promotional tour for *Academy*.

When I'd spoken to my agent to tell her no more auditions, she'd been shockingly understanding. She assumed it was a break after a long movie. I hadn't needed to tell her that it felt permanent. Maybe I'd change my mind. Maybe I wouldn't. All I knew was that as soon as I'd taken it off the table, I felt free again.

Not that I had any idea what I wanted to do from here. Maddox was right that I was in a position to wait for inspiration to strike.

So, I settled in, even going as far as bringing Maddox to my house in LA to pack up things to take back to Savannah. The first thing I'd grabbed was the picture Maddox had drawn for me in college. It deserved a place of honor in Gran's house.

But otherwise, the house in LA had felt cold. I'd spent years there alone after my second divorce, and the thought of it made me sick. When I told Maddox I wanted to sell it, he told me to do whatever I wanted. We could get a place in LA for when either of us had to be there for work. I'd gotten a real estate agent the next day to put it on the market. That house was old Josie. I'd get something new when I figured out who I was going forward.

The best part about being in town the rest of the summer was getting to spend more time with Marley and Lila. They drove down to hang out with me and Maddox, and we drove up there. We planned Lila's wedding, which she and Cole had decided would take place at the Chapel on UGA's campus next year. It was fitting since that was where they'd met.

And as the last rays set on July, I was finishing up the final pages of my mother's book with tears in my eyes.

"Josie," Maddox's voice called through the house.

"Back here," I said with a sniffle.

"Is everything okay?" He stepped through the back door and out onto the porch.

I closed the book. "I finished."

"How was it?"

"Sad," I said softly. "I need to talk to my mom."

"Aren't you having dinner with her tomorrow?"

"Yeah. I'm going to go over there now though."

"Want me to come with?"

I stood and pressed a kiss to his lips. "I love you, but no. Stay here. I made Gran's mac and cheese. It's in the oven on warm."

He groaned. "You know the way to my heart."

"Through your stomach," I said with a laugh.

"Just you."

We kissed again, and then I headed out the door with the book tucked under my arm. When I arrived back at my mom's home, I looked at it completely differently than I had all those summers I grew up here. It wasn't the bright future for my mom. The place she'd escaped her responsibility. The house was a prison. And I had no idea why she'd kept it.

I knocked once on the door and then stepped inside. "Mom?"

"Josie?" My mom stepped out of the kitchen, dressed to the nines, as always, with a martini glass in her hand. "Is everything okay? We're not supposed to have dinner until tomorrow."

I didn't say anything. I just walked across the living room and enveloped my mother in a hug. She made a sound just short of shock before she put her arm around me.

"What's going on? Are you and Maddox okay? Because you know I will skin him alive if he hurts you."

"Yes," I said on a laugh. "We're great. I just ... I finished the journal." I held it up, so she could see it. "I got to the end."

"Oh," she whispered. "Well, took you long enough. I thought you'd read it right away."

I chuckled. "I was busy. And it was ... heavy."

"Let's go outside. Do you want a drink?"

"You know what? I really do."

She smiled. A soft, genuine smile. "That's my girl."

She poured me a martini, and we took the drinks out to the pool. We took a seat on the lounge chairs under an umbrella.

"So, you know my whole story."

"He hit you," I forced myself to say.

My mother nodded. "Yes."

"You chose him after Dad wouldn't take you back, and then he made you suffer for your choice. He hit you for years. And I never knew. How ... how did you survive? Why didn't you leave?"

"You read why."

"He wouldn't let you leave."

"Abuse never starts out with physical pain. It starts out with psychological torture. With destroying your worth and your financial success and everything you know until all you have is him." Her voice wasn't weak. It was strong. Even recollecting what she'd gone through with him, she wasn't that weak person anymore. "And then, when he hits you, you think you deserve it. You made him do these things. If only you'd been more or better or some unattainable thing, then you would have been enough, and he wouldn't have raised a hand to you."

I choked on tears. "You didn't deserve that."

"No, I didn't, and it was many years before I realized that. But I knew all along that I wouldn't let it happen to you."

"That's why you gave Dad custody."

"Yes."

"And I only came back in the summers because Edward was gone. It was the only time you were safe."

"Yes. I could have left in the summer, but I didn't know what he'd do to you if I left. So, I didn't risk it. I couldn't risk it."

I took her hand in mine. "Thank you. Thank you for protecting me, even when I didn't understand what you were doing. Even when I resented you for it."

"Josie, I love you."

"I love you too, Mom." I squeezed her hand through tear-blurred eyes.

She held her martini glass aloft. "To freedom."

"To freedom," I agreed.

We clinked glasses and drank deeply of the gin.

"So," I asked as casually as possible, "did you do it?"

My mom arched an eyebrow at me. "Be more specific."

"You know … did you kill him?"

That had always been the rumor circulating. Half the time, I thought it was utterly ridiculous. Half the time, I knew the rumors had to come from somewhere. Usually, I'd assumed it was jealous sycophants who wanted my mother's money. But after reading the journal, it was entirely unclear exactly what had happened. Edward had been into prescription drugs. He'd done a lot of opioids. Overdoses were common.

My mom laughed. "Ah, I was waiting for this. What do you think?"

What did I think? I stared at my beautiful mother. My mirror. Could I have done it? I really didn't think so, and I didn't think she could do it either.

"No. I don't think you did it."

"Good. I'm glad, darling," she said, patting my hand. "I like to hear that. The rumors and all the slander don't matter. Only what you think does."

"I have an idea. A wild idea."

"What's that?"

"I want to make this into a movie."

She laughed. "What into a movie?"

"This journal. Your life. I can see it all on the big screen. I know exactly how I'd play it."

"You want to make my life a movie?" she asked, momentarily shocked.

"Yes. I want to direct it and make it into something valuable. Maddox reminded me that I always wanted to direct and that I was interested in women's stories. The ones that weren't being told. What better than *your* story?"

"That boy is good for you."

"He is," I agreed easily. "What do you think?"

"I say yes with two conditions."

I waited for the ball to drop. For her to request something ridiculous, as she always had when I was a kid. I hadn't known then that those requests were to keep me safe from Edward, but I'd hated her for them. Though I was learning to forgive and move on from the trauma of my childhood, I couldn't stop the involuntary reaction.

"What's that?"

"For one, you play me."

I relaxed at those words. Then, I laughed. "Me? No, I was going to direct."

"Directors can be the star too, Josephine. And you, my darling daughter, are both."

She was right, of course. There were plenty of actors who directed. It wouldn't be unusual. And ... the thought intrigued me. I'd have to step into my mother's shoes. Could I do that? Could anyone else do it better?

I nodded. "Okay. I'll do it. What's the second request?"

"You have to get your father's permission too."

Of course. It was both of their stories. It was only fair that I ask him too.

"I will absolutely do that."

"Good. I always knew that I was meant for the big screen," she said with a wink.

And we both giggled at that.

I felt the bridge finally rebuilding between us, and this movie was only going to bring us closer. And I couldn't wait.

30

ATLANTA
PRESENT

"What if he says no?" I asked, chewing on my hair in Maddox's truck as we got off I-85 and headed toward my dad's house.

"Then, he says no."

"I don't have another idea."

"You'll come up with another idea," he assured me. "You were off for no time at all and had *this* idea. I'm sure if you gave yourself another week, you'd have a new idea."

I shrugged. "Maybe."

"And he's not going to say no. It's not like you're going to show him in a negative light."

"No ... just Edward."

"Personally, I think he wouldn't care if everyone saw Edward as the villain."

I glanced at him. "Not speaking from experience, are you?"

He squeezed my hand. "No idea what you're talking about."

"Sure. Sure," I said with a laugh.

Even with Maddox's words in my head, I couldn't stop the nerves as we parked in front of Dad's house. I grabbed the book and shouldered my bag before hopping out of the car and walking to the front door.

Maddox knocked, and Dad opened the door, holding a paintbrush. I just shook my head.

"I'm in the middle of a breakthrough. Come in. Come in. Hurry."

Maddox and I shared a look and then followed Dad inside. As eccentric as ever.

He was working in my old bedroom. A canvas was on the ground, and there was paint everywhere. It half-looked like he'd been suspended from something and thrown paint from the ceiling. Luckily, he'd had the fore-thought to put a sheet over the bed.

"Dad, what the hell are you doing?"

"Genius," he said without a hint of joking.

Maddox turned his head to the side. "I like it. It kind of reminds me of the kaleidoscopes we had as kids. If you look at it from another perspectives, it's a different picture."

"Yes, yes!" my dad said. "He gets it."

I hugged the book to my chest and waited for them to be finished. It was another half hour, in which Maddox got paint all over his shirt and in his curly hair. I picked my feet up and backed farther away from the mess.

"Okay. That's it for today. Let's go into the living room."

"Dad, you should change."

"Right you are."

He disappeared into the back and came out a few minutes later in fresh clothing. Maddox had stripped out of his shirt and dug through his duffel to find a fresh one. Finally, we all sat down in the living room. Dad had gotten us all beers.

"What's this all about? I'm glad you're here, but you didn't seem like yourself on the phone."

I took a deep breath and launched into my pitch. It was harder to ask this of my dad, considering he was the first victim of the entire ordeal. I knew he didn't want to relive what had happened or have hundreds or thousands or even millions of other people to relive it with him. But I needed his permission before I proceeded.

At the end, Dad was struck silent. He ran a hand across his beard and then held his hand out. "That's the journal?"

"A copy. I had one made for you." I put it in his hand. "She loved you, Dad. And ... she was protecting me the best she could. I believe that now."

"And Edward really ... hit her?" he asked. His hand clenched tight around the book, his knuckles white at the thought.

"Yes," I whispered.

"Did he ever raise a hand to you?"

I shook my head. "No. I barely saw him when I was there. That's why she asked me to come in the summers —because he was gone. I had no idea until I read the journal."

He sighed heavily. "I wish she'd told me."

There was so much weight in those words. An entire lifetime of what could have been.

"Me too."

The silence was heavy, but I let it hang. Let my dad process everything I'd told him. It was a lot to take in. It had been for me, and he'd been there for half of it.

Finally, he met my gaze again. "And you want to make this into a movie?"

"I do. I feel like I'm finally following my passion again."

"All right," he said with a nod. "I can't guarantee I'll read it. I don't know if I want to know all of Rebecca's inner thoughts. But I won't stop you from creating. Not when you've done so much for me all these years."

I jumped to my feet and wrapped my arms around my dad's shoulders. "I love you, Dad."

"I love you too, sweetheart. Just promise to come back with Maddox more often."

I laughed and swiped at my tears. I met Maddox's gaze, and he nodded. "Definitely."

"I'd be happy to," Maddox agreed.

"Well, when do you start?" Dad asked.

"Now."

Maddox coughed up a lungful of dust. "Jesus, has *anyone* gone through the stuff in this attic ever?"

"Not for years," my mom said. She waved her hand in front of her face to clear the dust.

"Rebecca, allow me to introduce you to the show *Hoarders*."

I cracked up. "Mom isn't a hoarder. This is just the attic, Maddox."

"Just because she can hide her hoarding doesn't make it any less hoarding."

"Well, won't you thank me when you don't have to do all new costumes for the movie?" Mom said.

Maddox snorted and then started coughing again.

"Go downstairs if you can't handle the dust," I said as I navigated the towers of boxes in my mother's attic.

Developing my mother's journal to a film was an endeavor like I'd never gone through. I'd had to fall heavily back into things that I'd learned at SCAD when I was first trying to get into directing. I'd reached out to my film advisor from college about the direction. We'd set up weekly meetings for consultations on the project.

But Maddox had been right. What really got me through was my experience on *Academy*. All of the directors I'd worked with on different episodes of the show. The hours of rehearsing lines and filming and acting and dealing with technical direction. The millions of little things that I'd acquired over the years were now a fount of knowledge in my head.

Then there was Maddox.

Because he had worked on a host of blockbuster films and seen his fair share of direction. Plus, he had the opposite expertise of me. He knew post-production and angles and settings. He saw the half of the picture that I was missing.

Eventually, a script had been shaped out of the journal. Scenes came into focus. Everything fit together like the ingredients for Gran's perfect biscuit recipe.

I'd phoned in some favors to get actors in for the roles. The scheduling was a *nightmare*, to say the least. But I was excited that at least I'd gotten Iris in for a part. The role of my dad was easily the most difficult to cast, and Edward was the easiest. A young *me* had also been challenging, but officially, the film was set. And we were doing everything to not go over budget.

Which was why we were digging through my mom's boxes.

"Found it!" I cheered.

I ripped open a box to find an array of tulle, big puffy sleeves, oversize blazers with shoulder pads, mom jeans, velvet track suits, and more.

"Oh my God," I gasped. I held up a ruffled hot-pink dress with massive sleeves. "Why did you keep all of this?"

"I hate getting rid of things," my mom said. "And that was my senior prom dress, mind you."

I burst into giggles. Even Maddox chuckled.

"Here's a box of Edward's clothes too." She removed clothes that looked like they had come straight out of a John Hughes film. "Well, will it do?"

"1988 has never looked so good."

"Ready?" Maddox whispered against my ear.

I leaned back into him, soaking up his warmth and encouragement. He'd shown me the sets he'd designed for his visual effects studio on his computer. I'd oohed and aahed in amazement that I was going to get to use the studio for the cost of utilities and his assistants. I'd tried to pay him in some way multiple times, but he'd winked and carried me to bed.

"Ready," I said.

The lights flicked on, and the LED screen projected back the landscape of Forsyth Park. My heart hammered. It looked *just* like we were in the park, only a few miles away. As if I could reach out and touch it. I'd seen the system used to make *Academy*, but that had been a Faerie world. It hadn't been real. This felt … even more incredible because I couldn't tell the difference.

"You're brilliant."

"Thanks. I know."

I pushed him, and he just laughed.

"Don't get cocky."

He nipped at my ear. "You like me that way."

"In the bedroom."

He snorted. "Fair. Are you ready for your first scene, Director?"

I got ecstatic at that word. "I'm fucking ready."

I'd been in hair and makeup all morning, re-creating my mother's infamous '80s hair. The wild curls with more volume than I'd thought was possible. I was in a simple dress that set off my eyes and layers of makeup. And I was ready.

I stepped into the room for my directorial debut. A clapperboard cracked in front of me.

"*Montgomery House.* Scene one. Take one."

And then I was walking forward through Forsyth Park, taking the short trek to Abercorn and getting my first look at Edward's family's historical home—Montgomery House. I'd have a voice-over speaking during this opening scene. But for now, it was just me wandering through Savannah and staring up at the house that had haunted me.

"Cut," I called and turned around. "How'd it go?"

I dashed back over to look at the film and watched that momentous first walk, giddy with anticipation. Tears came to my eyes all over again. It was really happening. Really, really happening.

I shot Maddox a thumbs-up, and he nodded his head. I glanced over and found my dad, of all people, walking into the room. And standing next to him was *my mom*.

My eyes rounded, and I jumped out of the director's seat and straight for them. "Hey, this is a surprise!"

"I didn't want to miss your first big day," Mom said.

"And I ... read the journal you left at my house," Dad said.

"Really?"

"So, I called Rebecca to ask if she wouldn't mind if I came over to discuss it with her. And she invited me to the set."

I looked between my parents. "You went over to Montgomery House?"

"Well, I didn't go inside," Dad admitted. "Haven't wanted to be in that house in a couple decades." He laughed, brushing it off. "But it was good to talk to your mom here."

My mom's eyes were only for my dad. After all this time, did she *still* love him? They hadn't spoken since my college graduation. I was sure it had been longer than that since they'd said a civil word to one another. My movie was doing more good than I'd even known possible.

"I'm glad you're both here. I love to see you two in the same place. Dad, you're free to come down anytime. Maddox and I have a guest bedroom too, you know?"

"Sure, sweetheart." He kissed my cheek.

"We didn't mean to interfere," Mom said.

My dad finally took in what I was wearing. His jaw dropped, and he glanced at my mom. "Is that the dress?"

She nodded. "Yes, it was mine."

I ran my hand down the front of it, feeling like I was living in a dream. My parents talking. My parents smiling. My parents ... united.

"What's important about this one? I picked it because it was the plainest."

"Your mom was wearing that the day we met," my dad admitted. "I still remember what you looked like that day."

My mom blushed. My mother, the indominable Rebecca Charlotte Montgomery, *blushed*.

"I don't quite look like that anymore," she said with a laugh.

My dad tilted his head. "You haven't changed a bit."

And my mom giggled. As if she were that schoolgirl all over again. As if it were 1988 and she was meeting Charlie for the first time.

I bit my lip and tried not to giggle too. "Well, I should get back. I need to do another take or two. Make yourselves comfortable."

"Thanks, sweetheart." My dad kissed my cheek.

Mom waved, and then they headed to seats to watch.

Maddox arched an eyebrow at me. "What was that about?"

"I'm not sure yet," I admitted. "But ... all good things."

"They deserve it."

"So do we," I said and then kissed him.

"That's a wrap!" I called a few short weeks later.

Everyone cheered noisily, jumping up and down and dancing in circles.

We'd worked day and night on *Montgomery House*. I'd be up before the sun for hair and makeup and stay long past midnight, going over the footage for the day. Maddox had to be in LA for another movie soon, and we'd tried to rush to meet his deadline. We'd still have to take weeks in post-production, but at least we'd gotten through with everything we needed for the studio. And all the scenes we needed were now officially on film.

In lieu of a fancy party on River Street, my mom had invited everyone over to the *real* Montgomery House for an '80s-themed party. A few hours after we wrapped up, the entire cast and crew showed up, dressed in '80s digs. They marveled at the real house that had inspired the movie. After a few drinks, people ditched their '80s outfits for swimsuits, splashing in the pool and singing boisterously to the '80s music my mom had insisted we listen to.

But what was most shocking was my *dad* showing up in a full '80s getup, complete with a mullet.

"Dad, you *didn't*!" I gasped.

He laughed. "I never had one in the '80s. I thought, why not?"

"It's truly terrible, Charlie," my mom said. She fluffed the shorter strands. "You didn't quite get the front to stick up enough."

"Mom!"

She grinned at me. "What? We found them incredibly attractive at the time, Josephine."

"Did you have eyes?"

My dad winked at me. "Business in the front. Party in the back."

"Maddox, if you ever …"

He held his hands up. "I would never think about it."

"How does it feel to be finished with filming?" Dad asked.

"Amazing. It feels like the best thing I've ever done in my entire life."

"We can't wait to see it. Can we, Charlie?"

Maddox and I shared a look. Dad had been coming in a lot more often to watch filming. He hadn't said anything about what was happening between him and Mom, but I could guess what I *thought* was happening. Especially considering he'd used the guest bedroom at our house twice and then not stayed there since. But I wasn't going to pressure them to say more about what was going on before they were ready. It had taken them thirty years to get back to a place where they didn't hate each other. I was excited that they could be in the same room. That Dad could ever *be* in Edward's old house after everything that had happened.

"Mom," I said softly, "did you ever think of selling Montgomery House?"

"No," she said decisively.

"Why not? It has so many bad memories."

"Because then Edward would have won." She nodded once. "The house is mine. I earned it."

Rebecca Charlotte Montgomery surveyed the house that had been her undoing. The house that had shaped her entire life. The house she lived in alone with the weight of her bad reputation on her shoulders. And she smiled.

I'd written, directed, and acted in a movie about this very house, and I'd never really understood what had kept my mom here until this moment. The house was just a house. The memories were in the past. No one was going to run her out of this town. She deserved to be here. And anyone who said otherwise didn't matter.

The Montgomery House had haunted me long enough.

Now, it was just home.

31

SAVANNAH
PRESENT

I'd been here before.

Standing behind a cinema screen with the biggest project of my life. The last time, I'd been all nerves. Something had been missing from the film, but I hadn't had enough experience to know what it was at the time. I had given up on that dream for so long and washed my hands of that day.

Now, I was here again. The nerves were still there, but certainly not the same ones. *Montgomery House* was perfect. Or as perfect as I could get it. If no one else liked it, then I'd done my very best, and I knew it for the masterpiece it was. I was confident in the movie and what Maddox and I had accomplished together.

Because this was as much his triumph as it was mine. I was certain that I never could have done what I'd done with him. Together, we were a formidable team.

"This looks good on you," Maddox said, sliding a hand down my hip.

"The dress that Amelia made for me?"

"Confidence."

I grinned back at him. "It's the best that I can do. I love the movie. I cry every time I watch it. No matter how many times I watch it. I even saw you shed a tear."

He brought my mouth up to his. "It's perfectly you, Jos."

"Thank you for all your help."

"It was fun."

And he was right. It had been *fun*. Even in the stressful months when we'd had to flit between Savannah and LA while he was working on the next superhero film. Even in the hours of post-production when I had been certain we'd have to do reshoots. Even through the tears that it wouldn't come together, I would always rather be working on it than anything else. Working for myself than another director.

I'd made a speech before the showing of *Montgomery House*. It was the only showing there would be since I'd sent it out to all the major film festivals—Cannes, Sundance, Toronto, Berlin, Venice, and so many more. I couldn't officially premiere it before I was accepted, but all of my friends had wanted to see it. So, I'd rented out Trustees Theater for the night—the same exact theater where my first film had premiered at the SCAD Savannah Film Festival a decade earlier—and invited all of my friends in to see it.

No red carpet.

No celebrities.

Nothing special.

Just me with a microphone, thanking everyone for

coming and welcoming them to my favorite movie, based on a true story—*Montgomery House.*

My mom and dad were in the first row, holding hands. They hadn't made anything official, but I had a feeling it was only a matter of time. Lila and Cole sat next to Derek and Marley. Amelia was a row behind them with her cousin Marina. No Ash Talmadge in sight. My SCAD film advisor was in the audience. Martin was there with his latest girlfriend. Iris and the rest of the cast and crew, who had come into Savannah for the showing, took up the back half of the audience. All of my favorite people in one place.

The credits rolled, and to my utter shock, every single person in the stadium got to their feet and applauded. My hand went to my mouth at the standing ovation. Tears in my eyes.

Maddox gave me a little shove. "Go on. Accept everything you deserve."

I laughed and stumbled forward. The cheers only got louder when I appeared. Maddox jogged out a microphone to me.

"Thank you. Thank you so much. I couldn't be happier that each and every one of you was in attendance for the first official viewing of *Montgomery House.* We're still waiting to hear about any of the film festivals and a possible theatrical release, but I wanted all of you to see it first. Special shout-out to my mother, Rebecca Montgomery, who the script is based off. And all the cast and crew, who put their hearts and souls into it. Especially my boyfriend, Maddox Nelson, who, without his genius, this never would have been possible."

I gestured offstage and waved for him to come out. He hated the spotlight, but he walked out with all the confidence that I knew him capable of. He waved at our friends and family as they cheered me on, and together, we took a small bow.

Maddox took the microphone from me and stepped back. "Ladies and gentlemen, Josephine Reynolds!"

The crowd went wild at my introduction. I bowed again, thanking them all profusely.

When the room finally cleared, it was just my friends and family backstage. I hugged them all and agreed to go out on River Street with them to celebrate.

"Mom? Dad? You in?" I asked.

They laughed and shook their heads.

"All you, sweetheart," Dad said, kissing my cheek.

"We're going to call it an early night," Mom said with a wink.

"Ew, I'm still your daughter," I said but couldn't help laughing.

"We love you."

"I love you too. Both of you."

My mother was still the ridiculous, over-the-top woman she'd always been. But when she looked at my dad, she was just a girl again. And the feeling seemed to be mutual. I was happy for them.

We waved good-bye and then grabbed jackets and trekked down the cobblestone streets toward River Street. Our friends headed into the nearest bar, but Maddox tugged me away. I laughed but jogged across the street to lean against the railing and look out at the paddleboat coming in.

"Do you remember our first time at this spot?"

"It was our first kiss," I said automatically. "A perfect first kiss."

"It was. I was hoping to steal another one tonight."

"I do believe you've earned a kiss tonight," I said with a mischievous look on my face. "Maybe more than a kiss."

"You read my mind," he said.

Then, he removed a box from his jacket. My mouth dropped open as he fell to one knee before me in the exact spot where we'd had our first kiss all those years ago. He opened the box, and inside was a glittering diamond ring that I recognized all too well—Gran's ring.

"Josie Reynolds, will you do me the honor of marrying me?"

"Maddox, oh my God, yes! Yes, yes, yes!"

He rose to his feet and plucked the ring out of the box. When he slid it into place, it fit perfectly.

"It's Gran's," I said, a sob getting caught in my throat.

"She gave it to me before she went into the hospital," he admitted. "Said that I would know who it belonged to. It was always meant for you."

"I love you so much," I said, crushing our lips together.

"I love you too. And I want to spend the rest of my life with you."

"Forever," I agreed easily. "You're never going to find anyone else to make those biscuits how you like them."

He laughed. "That is a bonus, to be sure. But it's just your incredible, brilliant self that made me fall for you."

"Brilliant," I said with a laugh.

He cupped my face in his hands. "You, Josie, are brilliant. That movie was brilliant. Everything you do is brilliant. I'm going to say it every day for the rest of our lives."

I kissed him again, slow and languid. "I find that acceptable."

"Hey! Are y'all coming?" Marley called across the street.

Lila was waving from the doorway.

I held up my left hand. "I'm engaged!"

They both screamed and ran straight into traffic. We all laughed as they nearly got hit by a car while crossing the street to get a look at my ring. They gushed over it for a few minutes, congratulating the both of us and then dragging us into the bar for rounds of celebratory drinks.

My eyes drifted to Maddox's, and he reached for me. Our hands slid together, finding each other, as we always had so often in the past.

He pressed a kiss to my ring. "Mine," he whispered.

I'd been his for a long time. And now, I'd be his forever.

EPILOGUE
CANNES

Next Year

The French Riviera was every inch as beautiful as I remembered it being, but twice as beautiful because of the reason we were here..

"So, how does it feel?" Maddox asked as we strolled hand in hand down the boardwalk.

"Like a fairy tale."

"And yet it is your reality."

"Still hard to believe. I mean, we're in Cannes, and I still can't believe the movie is *in* the Cannes Film Festival," I said, gesturing to the glamorous coastal city surrounding us.

When I'd gotten the call that I was accepted into Cannes, I'd cried like a baby. I sat on the floor in the master bedroom and sobbed incoherently until Maddox threatened to take me to a hospital. When I'd told him the truth, he'd picked me up off of the floor and twirled me around until I was laughing instead of crying.

I'd gotten into Sundance too. And Toronto. And Berlin. And Venice. And a dozen other smaller festivals. I'd cried every time. All my dreams were coming true, and a year earlier, it had sounded impossible.

My film wouldn't premiere for another hour, but there were already rumors that I might sweep the first-time film award. I was giddy and terrified at the idea. I'd find out at the end of the festival if I won, but it didn't even matter. Just being chosen as a feature film for the festival was life-changing.

"I'm proud of you, you know?" Maddox said.

"I'm proud of myself."

"That's what matters. You went after what you wanted, and look at how the universe manifested for you. It's been incredible to witness."

"Thank you."

"Just glad to be along for the ride."

"You have Oscars, and you're just along for the ride."

He laughed. "Well, maybe you'll have one too."

"Then, I'd just need a Tony and a Grammy, and I'd be an EGOT."

Maddox shot me a skeptical look as we headed back up to street level. "Can you even sing?"

"Oh God, no," I said, bursting into laughter. "I guess I'd just be happy with an Oscar."

"Just," he said with a snort.

"Hey, you said I could do anything."

"I stand by that." He pulled me to a stop and pressed a kiss to my lips. "You can do whatever you put your mind to, and I'm the lucky guy who gets to be here for it all.

Because I have exactly what I want right here. Everything else is icing on the cake."

We kissed again, drowning in each other. It was crazy to think that we'd be married at the end of the year. Cole and Lila were having a small ceremony this summer that I would be a bridesmaid at, and then she'd be one at mine. I couldn't wait for all of us to be coupled up.

The only person I wasn't sure about was Amelia. I still had hopes that she and Ash could work it out … for her sake, of course. Personally, I thought she could do better, but she'd loved him her entire life. I'd have to wait and see how they could come back from what had happened at the wrap party.

"Okay, lovebirds," my dad said with one hand in the pocket of his linen pants and the other around my mom's waist.

"Leave them be, Charlie. I'm happy for them," Mom said.

I beamed, leaving Maddox's side to hug both of my parents. Dad had moved back to Savannah for the first time since I had been a kid. He and Mom weren't officially living together since he'd opened a new art studio in town, but they might as well have been. I'd never seen my mother so happy. Or my dad really either. I believed in second chances. And if anyone deserved it, they did.

"I'm so glad that y'all are here for my big day," I said.

My mom swished her big ballgown. "I'm ready for your triumph."

We all linked elbows and then entered the back of the theater. We were quickly whisked away to our seats to watch. Maddox kept his hand tight in mine the entire time. I couldn't stop shaking, watching my masterpiece and waiting for it to all be a dream.

But at the end, the audience applauded. They came to their feet for a standing ovation. I forced back the tears that came so easily. I was meant to be here.

I was swept into the crowd of industry professionals. Everyone wanted a minute of my time. And I was happy to oblige. Maddox disappeared at some point. Too many people for him. But I always knew where he was, and we worked like this.

Everyone thought it was genius that, at the end, I hadn't told whether or not Rebecca had actually killed her husband. It was left up to the imagination. And everyone had their own theory. They were as bad as the town gossips back home in Savannah. Half believed she had done it, and half believed he'd overdosed on his own. I smiled and let them come to their own conclusions.

My mother loved being in the spotlight as well. When I'd asked her to come, I'd been afraid that people would be mean to her. I'd warned her that it might be traumatic to have to continue relive it over and over, but my mother wasn't anyone else. She was perfectly comfortable in every setting. She had no fears that these people could do anything to her that hadn't already been done.

My mom finally extracted me from the crowd, and we headed back down the boardwalk. Maddox and my dad strode a few steps behind us. Maddox had started going to my dad's new studio every weekend, and I loved to see their friendship grow.

"Mom, I wanted to ... thank you." I smiled at her. "For

giving me the journal, for trying to fix our broken relationship, for letting me make the movie."

"I'm so glad to have my daughter back. I did it all for you."

"I know," I said with a smile. "But also, for you."

My mother smiled, soaking in the Mediterranean air. "Maybe a little for me."

"Edward kept us apart for so long. It's horrible to say, but I'm glad he's gone."

"Me too. He was not the man that I thought I knew. I never would have forgiven him if he'd hurt you."

"I hardly ever saw him," I said. "He was gone every summer."

"Yes," she said softly. Softer than I'd heard her in an age. "But you were starting to look like me, and he noticed."

"What?" I asked in confusion.

"Don't you remember? You came up for Marley and Lila's dance recital the summer before you turned twelve." Her voice was calm and controlled, but her eyes were bright. They asked me to remember.

"I think so. He died that summer, right?"

"He took one look at you and knew that you were going to grow up to look just like me. He saw the young woman I'd been when we first met. A child. Another man's child."

"Mom, what are you saying?"

She squeezed my hand tight. "I'd do anything to protect you, Josephine."

Our eyes met, and I nearly froze in place at the look on her face. She'd said those words to me before, but I'd never given them much thought. In all of the time that I'd worked on this movie, I'd tried to show both sides. I wanted the audience divided on what had happened between Rebecca and Edward. The division made it viral and intense.

But all along, I'd known that my mom hadn't done it. Edward had died of an overdose. Tragic but all of his own doing.

Now, my certainty wavered.

"Mom?"

She patted my cheek, and a smile came to her face. "When you have a child, you'll understand."

"Understand what?" I whispered.

"That you'd kill to keep them safe."

I stopped in my tracks, but my mom kept walking. Dad jogged to catch up to her. But I was frozen in place. Maddox took my arm.

"Everything all right?" he asked. "You look like you saw a ghost."

"Yes." I cleared my throat. "Yes, everything's fine." I kissed him, shaking off my uncertainty and laying my head against his shoulder.

I'd tell Maddox eventually. But right now, I bore the secret that my mother had grappled with these last twenty years. The thing she'd never uttered to anyone. That she'd gotten away with for two decades. The truth that she'd buried as thoroughly as her first husband.

She had done it.

And she'd gotten away with it.

THE END

ACKNOWLEDGMENTS

Second to None was a dream to write. I literally feel like I wrote it in a fever dream. I've been waiting to write this story for so long. I had the idea for Rebecca for years and it solidified when I listened to Taylor Swift's song *The Next Great American Dynasty*, which was so similar to the idea I already had. I knew I had to write it! Intertwining Rebecca's story with Josie and Maddox's love story meant everything to me. Plus, he's my first real introvert just like my husband who I cannot thank enough for helping me with this novel.

The soundtrack to this book was: Taylor Swift's Speak Now album especially *Better Than Revenge* and *Haunted*, Ed Sheeran's Equal album especially *The Joker and the Queen*, *Loved You a Little* by The Maine, *Feels Like* by Gracie Adams, and *Want You Like That* by Charlotte Sands.